I0713348

MOUNTAIN OF
Evil

TS OMEGA TEAM
PREQUEL

SAMANTHA COLE
Suspenseful Seduction Publishing

To my brother, Jim. Love ya!

Acknowledgements

I'd like to thank the following people who have been a part of my two year literary journey:

My friends and family for all their support.

My beta readers:
Allena, Brandie, Charla, Debbie, Felisha, Jen, Jessica, Joanne, Julie, Katie, Kelle, and Milynn.
Love every one of you!

My editor, Eve—you're the best!

Judi Perkins of Concierge Literary Designs for an amazing cover that was just what I had hoped for.

My Sexy Six-Pack Sirens Facebook group for their shout outs, whip cracking, and everyday fun.
Y'all are the bomb!

And as always, last, but far from least, my readers. Without you, I would have never have come this far.

Who's Who and the History of Trident Security & The Covenant

***While not every character is in every book, these are the ones with the most mentions throughout the series. This guide will help keep readers straight about who's who.

Trident Security (TS) is a private investigative and military agency, co-owned by Ian and Devon Sawyer. With governmental and civilian contracts, the company got its start when the brothers and a few of their teammates from SEAL Team Four retired to the private sector. The original six-man team is referred to as the Sexy Six-Pack, as they were dubbed by Kristen Sawyer, née Anders, or the Alpha Team. Trident had since expanded and former members of the military and law enforcement have been added to the staff. The company is located on a guarded compound, which was a former import/export company cover for a drug trafficking operation in Tampa, Florida. Three warehouses on the property were converted into large apartments, the TS offices, gym, and bunk rooms. There is also an obstacle course, a Main Street shooting gallery, a helicopter pad, and more features necessary for training and missions.

In addition to the security business, there is a fourth warehouse that now houses an elite BDSM club, co-owned by Devon, Ian, and their cousin, Mitch Sawyer, who is the manager. A lot of time and money has gone into making The Covenant the most sought after membership in the Tampa/St. Petersburg area and beyond. Members are thoroughly vetted before being granted access to the elegant club.

There are currently over fifty Doms who have been appointed Dungeon Masters (DMs), and they rotate two or three shifts each throughout the month. At least four DMs are on duty at all times at various posts in the pit, playrooms, and the new garden, with an additional one roaming around. Their job is to ensure the safety of all the submissives in the club. They step in if a sub uses their safeword and the Dom in the scene doesn't hear or heed it, and make sure the equipment used in scenes isn't harming the subs.

The Covenant's security team takes care of everything else that isn't scene-related, and provides safety for all members and are essentially the bouncers. With the recent addition of the garden, and more private, themed rooms, the owners have expanded their self-imposed limit of 350 members. The fire marshal had approved them for 500 when the warehouse-turned-kink club first opened, but the cousins had intentionally kept that number down to maintain an elite status. Now with more room, they are increasing the membership to 500, still under the new maximum occupancy of 720.

Between Trident Security and The Covenant there's plenty of romance, suspense, and steamy encounters. Come meet the Sexy Six-Pack, their friends, family, and teammates.

The Sexy Six-Pack (Alpha Team) and Their Significant Others

- Ian "Boss-man" Sawyer: Devon and Nick's brother; retired Navy SEAL; co-owner of Trident Security and The Covenant; husband/Dom of Angelina (Angel).
- Devon "Devil Dog" Sawyer: Ian and Nick's brother; retired Navy SEAL; co-owner of Trident Security and The Covenant; husband/Dom of Kristen; father of John Devon "JD."
- Ben "Boomer" Michaelson: retired Navy SEAL; explosives and ordnance specialist; husband/Dom of Katerina; son of Rick and Eileen.
- Jake "Reverend" Donovan: retired Navy SEAL; temporarily assigned to run the West Coast team; sniper; fiancé/Dom of Nick; brother of Mike; Whip Master at The Covenant.
- Brody "Egghead" Evans: retired Navy SEAL; computer specialist; husband/Dom of Fancy.
- Marco "Polo" DeAngelis: retired Navy SEAL; communications specialist and back up helicopter pilot; husband/Dom of Harper; father to Mara.

- Nick "Junior" Sawyer: Ian and Devon's brother; current Navy SEAL; fiancé/submissive of Jake.
- Kristen "Ninja-girl" Sawyer: author of romance/suspense novels; wife/submissive of Devon; mother of "JD."
- Angelina "Angie/Angel" Sawyer: graphic artist; wife/submissive of Ian.
- Katerina "Kat" Michaelson: dog trainer for law enforcement and private agencies; wife/submissive of Boomer.
- Millicent "Harper" DeAngelis: lawyer; wife/submissive of Marco; mother of Mara.
- Francine "Fancy" Maguire: baker; fiancée/submissive of Brody.

Extended Family, Friends, and Associates of the Sexy Six-Pack

- Mitch Sawyer: Cousin of Ian, Devon, and Nick; co-owner/manager of The Covenant, Dom to Tyler and Tori.
- T. Carter: US spy and assassin; works for covert agency Deimos; Dom of Jordyn.
- Jordyn Alvarez: US spy and assassin; member of covert agency Deimos; submissive of Carter.
- Tyler Ellis: Stockbroker; lifestyle switch—Dom to Tori; submissive to Mitch.
- Tori Freyja: K9 trainer for veterans in need of assistance/service dogs; submissive to Mitch and Tyler.

- Parker Christiansen: owner of New Horizons Construction; husband/Dom of Shelby; adoptive father of Franco and Victor.
- Shelby Christiansen: stay-at-home mom; two-time cancer survivor; wife/submissive of Parker; adoptive mother of Franco and Victor.
- Curt Bannerman: retired Navy SEAL; owner of Halo Customs, a motorcycle repair and detail shop; husband of Dana; stepfather of Ryan, Taylor, Justin, and Amanda. Lives in Iowa.
- Dana Prichard-Bannerman: teacher; widow of retired SEAL Eric Prichard; wife of Curt; mother of Ryan, Taylor, Justin, and Amanda. Lives in Iowa.
- Jenn "Baby-girl" Mullins: college student; goddaughter of Ian; "niece" of Devon, Brody, Jake, Boomer, and Marco; father was a Navy SEAL; parents murdered.
- Mike Donovan: owner of the Irish pub, Donovan's; brother of Jake; submissive/boyfriend of Charlotte.
- Charlotte "Mistress China" Roth: Parole officer; Domme/girlfriend of Mike; Whip Master at The Covenant.
- Travis "Tiny" Daultry: former professional football player; head of security at The Covenant and Trident compound; occasional bodyguard for TS.
- Doug "Bullseye" Henderson: retired Marine; head of the Personal Protection Division of TS.

- Rick and Eileen Michaelson: Boomer's parents; guardians of Alyssa. Rick is a retired Navy SEAL.
- Charles "Chuck" and Marie Sawyer: Ian, Devon, and Nick's parents. Charles is a self-made real estate billionaire. Marie is a plastic surgeon involved with Operation Smile.
- Will Anders: Assistant Curator of the Tampa Museum of Art Kristen Anders's cousin.
- Dr. Roxanne London: pediatrician; Domme/wife (Mistress Roxy) of Kayla; Whip Master at Covenant.
- Kayla London: social worker; submissive/wife of Roxanne.
- Grayson and Remington Mann: twins; owners of Black Diamond Records; Doms/fiancés of Abigail; members of The Covenant.
- Abigail Turner: personal assistant at Black Diamond Records; submissive/fiancée of Gray and Remi.
- Chase Dixon: retired Marine Raider; owner of Blackhawk Security; associate of TS.
- Reggie Helm: lawyer for TS and The Covenant; Dom/husband of Colleen.
- Alyssa Wagner: teenager saved by Jake from an abusive father; lives with Rick and Eileen Michaelson.
- Carl Talbot: college professor; Dom and Whip Master at The Covenant.

The Omega Team and Their Significant Others

- Cain "Shades" Foster: retired Secret Service agent.
- Tristan "Duracell" McCabe: retired Army Special Forces
- Valentino "Romeo" Mancini: retired Army Special Forces; former FBI Hostage Rescue Team (HRT) member.
- Darius "Batman" Knight: retired Navy SEAL.
- Kip "Skipper" Morrison: retired Army; former LAPD SWAT sniper.
- Lindsey "Costello" Abbott: retired Marine; sniper.

Trident Support Staff

- Colleen McKinley-Helm: office manager of TS; wife/submissive of Reggie.
- Tempest "Babs" Van Buren: retired Air Force helicopter pilot; TS mechanic.
- Russell Adams: retired Navy; assistant TS mechanic.
- Nathan Cook: former computer specialist with the National Security Agency (NSA).

Members of Law Enforcement

- Larry Keon: Assistant Director of the FBI.
- Frank Stonewall: Special Agent in Charge of the Tampa FBI.
- Calvin Watts: Leader of the FBI HRT in Tampa.
- Colt Parrish: Major Case Specialist, Behavioral Analysis Unit.

The K9s of Trident

- Beau: An orphaned Lab/Pit mix, rescued by Ian. Now a trained K9 who has more than earned his spot on the Alpha Team.
- Spanky: A rescued Bullmastiff with a heart of gold, owned by Parker and Shelby.
- Jagger: A rescued Rottweiler trained as an assistance/service animal for Russell.
- FUBAR: A Belgian Malinois who failed aggressive guard dog training. Adopted by Babs.
- BDSM: Bravo, Delta, Sierra, and Mike, two Belgian Malinoises and two German shepherds, the new guard dogs at the Trident compound that Ian named using the military communication's alphabet.

Author's Note

The story within these pages is completely fictional but the concepts of BDSM are real. If you do choose to participate in the BDSM lifestyle, please research it carefully and take all precautions to protect yourself. Fiction is based on real life but real life is *not* based on fiction. Remember-Safe, Sane and Consensual!

Any information regarding persons or places has been used with creative literary license so there may be discrepancies between fiction and reality. The military missions and personal qualities of the members of the individual armed forces within have been created to enhance the story and, again, may be exaggerated and not coincide with reality.

The author has full respect for the members of the United States Military and the varied members of law enforcement and thanks them for their continuing service to making this country as safe and free as possible.

***Liberties were taken regarding the town of Ouray, Colorado, the surrounding mountains, points of interest, and topography for the sake of the story. Any discrepancies are intentional.

Chapter One

Click. Click. Click.

Resting her arms, Mallory Hart inspected the pictures of a bald eagle she'd just shot on her digital camera. Hiking in the San Juan Mountain range of the Rockies was one of the best places for her to shoot nature scenes, which she'd then upload to stock photo sites for sale. She currently had over a thousand of them on various websites, and the extra income helped pay for her college classes, textbooks, and supplies.

After taking a few more shots of the majestic bird soaring overhead, she glanced at her watch: 2:30 p.m. She had about another hour before she had to start back down the marked trail. It was approximately two miles to where she'd parked her six-year-old, gray Toyota Corolla. Her friends thought she was crazy to go hiking alone on Wednesdays, when she didn't have any classes scheduled, but she liked the solitude. It wasn't often she came across another hiker this far into the wilderness during the middle of the week, and she always made sure she didn't stray far from the main trail. Just in case she did run into trouble, in her backpack was the satellite phone her father, who was retired from the Marines, insisted she have, since it was difficult to get a cell signal sometimes. There were also two bottles of water, a few granola bars, a compass, and spare batteries for her camera. Clipped to her jeans was a container of bear repellent.

A scurrying occurred behind her, and Mallory spun around to try and spot the small animal that had caused it. Her gaze flickered around the brush and trees, but there was no creature in sight. High above her, birds sang and squirrels chittered. The unusually warm weather in the mountains for late March had brought some of the wildlife out of hibernation early.

Squatting down, she tried to see if a red fox, wolverine, or porcupine might be looking for food. The sound had been too big to be a chipmunk or squirrel, and too small for anything larger. She searched high and low. *Nothing.*

A breeze lifted her blonde hair off her shoulders, and an odd chill went down her spine, causing her to pull her lightweight jacket tighter around her body. She was in the middle of the wilderness, high on a dirt trail, surrounded by aspen, cottonwood, and evergreen trees, some shrubbery, and rocks, yet she felt as if she were being watched. There was a gentle, downward slope to the east, leading to the small lake, and a more precarious, upward one to the west. Scanning the area around her, nothing seemed out of the ordinary. She hoped like hell it wasn't a cougar or wolf. A bear would make a lot more noise than those two carnivores—especially if it didn't realize Mallory was there.

Deciding to start back toward the parking area, she

kept her eyes out for wildlife she could shoot with her camera and any that might be a threat. After glancing back over her shoulder a few times, she began to relax a little, and her mind went to what her boyfriend had planned for their date tonight. She'd been seeing Kevin McCarthy for a few weeks now, and things were starting to get serious. He wanted to take things further, however, Mallory was nervous about it. She wasn't a virgin, so that wasn't the problem, but she hadn't been lucky with men in that department. The boy she'd lost her virginity to at sixteen had been sweet while they'd dated, but he'd left her for a girl he met in college while Mallory was still a senior in high school. The only other guy she'd been with had been after high school graduation, and he'd dumped her shortly after she'd put out. She'd learned too late, he'd only been looking for another notch in his bedpost.

Those were the only two men she'd ever slept with. Number three might have been a guy in her freshman year of college, but she found out the bastard in her English Literature class had a bet with his friends he would be in her bed in less than a week of dating. Mallory had sworn off the opposite sex for a while after that, concentrating on her schoolwork and photography instead. After a year of not dating, she'd finally broken down after Kevin had pursued her for several weeks. But with her past history of dating jerks, she was now gun-shy about sleeping with him.

She'd only gone about a quarter of a mile on the winding trail, when she stopped short. There was bear scat in the middle of the path, and from the stench, it was recent. It had to be, because she'd have noticed it when she came that way fifteen or twenty minutes ago.

"Shit," Mallory mumbled to herself. The unintended pun was lost on her as her gaze darted around again. "The last thing I need is a fresh-out-of-hibernation momma bear with her cubs."

Another rustling sounded to her left, and she shifted in that direction. Again, she couldn't help but feel like someone was studying her. She hadn't seen any hikers in over forty-five minutes, and the last ones had been two middle-aged women who'd been out birdwatching, and they'd been a lot closer to the parking area.

Letting her camera hang from the strap around her neck, Mallory unclipped the bear spray from her belt loop and carefully continued down the path. Rounding another curve, she gasped and froze when a large figure stepped out from behind a tree. Her heart pounded in her ears as she stared at the burly man dressed in military-style clothing. His unruly dark hair needed a trim and so did his beard and mustache. A jagged, two-inch scar ran from his upper lip across his right cheek. He was over six feet tall and almost as wide. A large knife was sheathed and strapped to his leg. While she didn't see any other weapons, that blade was enough to scare the crap out of her. Mallory gripped her bear spray tighter as the man grinned at her.

"Hey there, pretty girl. I didn't mean to scare you." His leer belied his rumbling words.

Mallory tried not to show she was afraid. Swallowing hard, she hoped her voice sounded strong and unaffected by the fear coursing through her. She pasted a fake smile on her face. "It's okay. You just startled me is all."

"Uh-huh." The man stepped forward, and Mallory

moved backward. "I scared you. I can see it on your pretty face. What's your name?"

She knew better than to tell him the truth, so she answered the first name that popped in her head. "Susan." *Sorry for borrowing your name, Mom.*

"Susan. Pretty name for a pretty girl."

The way he kept calling her "pretty" sent shivers down her spine. He took another step closer, and her gut churned. "Thanks, but if you don't mind, I'm in a hurry. I'm meeting people back at the parking area."

An ugly sneer crossed his face. "Oh, I don't think anyone is waiting for you. I think you're lying, and I don't like when people lie to me."

When the creep moved even closer, she started to lift the bear spray, more than willing to press the red button if she had to. Suddenly two arms wrapped around her torso from behind, pinning her own arms to her side. She screamed as she was lifted off the ground, her body twisting, trying to get loose. The spray bottle dropped out of her hand as she flailed her arms and legs. The man in front of her laughed when she tried to kick him, and grabbed her ankles with his dirty paws, holding them to the side. Mallory opened her mouth to scream again, but her throat went dry, and her eyes widened when he unsheathed the huge knife and held it in front of her face.

"Stay quiet, pretty girl, or I'll cut you into little pieces."

Sitting in the cockpit of Trident Security's jet, Ian Sawyer stared out at the blue horizon above the gray clouds below. Beside him, his pilot, Conrad "CC" Chapman, a retired Air Force captain, was thankfully not in a talkative mood. They were flying the Omega team to Colorado for their final training mission before letting them loose without being under the watchful eyes of the six members of the original Trident team. The plan was to drop them in the wilderness with the bare-bones minimum of supplies and a two day hike back to civilization to see if all the months of bonding and training had paid off. With new governmental and civilian contracts and missions coming in weekly, Ian and his brother, Devon, who co-owned the private security company, had spent the past sixteen months or so putting together another cracker-jack team. In addition to a West Coast team, which was still in its infancy as well, they would no longer need to subcontract additional personnel for many of their missions and cases. But all of that was not in the forefront of Ian's mind.

Back in Tampa, another submissive from the BDSM community had gone missing, and it was probably only a matter of days before her mutilated body would be found at some public spot. Brenda Arliss would be the serial killer's twelfth victim, unless she'd disappeared under other circumstances, which Ian doubted. He and Devon, along with their cousin Mitch, also co-owned an elite, private, BDSM club, and were worried one of The Covenant's subs would be targeted before the FBI and TPD figured out who the killer was. Hell, just knowing any woman, sub or not, from his club or not, had been tortured like the victims had been burned in his chest.

Six weeks ago, one of the Doms from The Covenant had been brought in by the FBI for questioning but had been released due to insufficient evidence. A DNA test and the solid alibi of being under surveillance by the FBI when Gina Spinak, the eleventh victim, had been snatched, had assured his innocence. The Dom apparently also was able to account for his whereabouts for when several of the other women were abducted but was being stubborn about revealing the information unless it was absolutely necessary. Ian figured it was because he'd been with a submissive who was in the public eye, but he couldn't be sure. Either way, the man was no longer a suspect, but that meant the FBI/Tampa PD/Trident Security task force was back to square one—again. Despite the head of the local FBI's objections, TS had been brought in as consultants due to their connections and involvement in the lifestyle.

The door to the cockpit swung open, and Tempest "Babs" Van Buren stuck her head in. "Coffee? I'm making a new pot because Batman's is crap that's not fit for human consumption."

Babs, short for her nickname "Bad-ass bitch," had been an Air Force helicopter pilot who'd been assigned to assist Ian's SEAL Team Four and a Marine unit in Afghanistan years ago. Her moniker hadn't come from an attitude problem, but because she'd been one of the most talented and bravest helo pilots around. She'd received numerous commendations during her tours in the devil's sandbox, the last one being a Purple Heart after coming under heavy enemy fire while extracting a few Marines from enemy territory. The tail rotor of the helo had been hit and failed, but thanks to Babs's talent in the sky, they'd been able to get far enough away from the hot zone, before she had to do a hard landing. What the Marines who were with her hadn't known until after the crash was she'd taken two bullets in her left leg, shattering the tibia and fibula, yet she'd still managed to fly the disabled bird. The doctors might have been able to save her limb had it just been the initial injury, but further damage was done when they crash landed. After being rescued, she'd been flown straight to a military hospital in Germany, where all efforts were exhausted before they'd finally amputated the leg before sending her back to the States to recover.

Before the female captain had been released from the hospital here in the US, Ian had gone for a visit and offered her a job with Trident. Once she'd gotten over the shock that she was still going to be able to fly a helicopter for missions, she'd accepted. Now, when she wasn't piloting their MH-X Silent Hawk, a military-grade, stealth bird, she was also an ace mechanic and maintained their fleet of vehicles, along with new hire Russell Adams. Most people didn't even realize Babs used a prosthesis unless they saw it. After training with the Trident boys for the past few months, she was entering her first marathon since losing her leg, having completed several of them while still in the Air Force.

CC waved Babs off, but Ian stood, and when the woman stepped back into the cabin, he followed her to the rear of the jet where there was a fully stocked kitchen. The rich aroma of coffee, which couldn't be coming from any convenience store brand, hung in the air, tantalizing his nose and making his mouth water. He grinned. "What? You don't like sludge anymore? You used to suck that shit down in the sandbox."

She let out an unladylike snort. "That's because I had no choice. Here, I do." Opening a cabinet, she pulled out a bag of whole beans from the Death Wish Coffee

Company, dubbed "the world's strongest coffee" and a grinder he hadn't known was in there. "I made sure to hide my own stash on board."

"Damn, woman, you're a saint." Grabbing a clean mug, he handed it to her to fill.

"Saint Babs." She smirked as she poured the coffee and handed it back to him. "I kinda like that. Although, I'm sure all the dead popes would roll over in their tombs if I was canonized."

Taking a sip of the dark brew, Ian's eyes fluttered shut as his taste buds rejoiced. "Fuck, that's good. Hide it from the peons out there. They haven't earned it yet. Hell, they may never earn it. When we get back to Tampa, order a case of this and stash it in my office. It's almost better than sex." When Babs lifted an eyebrow at him, he shrugged. "I said almost."

"Uh-huh."

Shaking his head, Ian turned and studied his new team, who were scattered about the luxury jet's seating. They came from a variety of military branches and law enforcement agencies. Cain Foster was sleeping in one of the recliners. The former Secret Service agent was very experienced with flying all over the United States and could fall asleep on a plane before it'd even taxied down the runway. Ian had seen him doze through several flights only to wake up completely refreshed as soon as the landing gear was lowered. He'd been one of their first hires for Omega and had quickly risen to the top of their list of who would lead the team. In the end, they'd chosen him and Tristan "Duracell" McCabe, who was sitting on one of the couches reading a political thriller, to be co-leaders.

McCabe was a retired Army Ranger, who'd been shot in the arm a scant few weeks before his last tour in Afghanistan ended. He'd still been recovering from the wound when he'd come to work for Trident. Both men excelled at leadership, and had experience and knowledge the other didn't possess—Foster was skilled in personal protection and dealing with social settings, and McCabe was an ace when it came to desert and jungle warfare. Together, they'd been the perfect choice to lead the team.

Lindsey "Costello" Abbott and Logan "Cowboy" Reese were sitting at a table with a backgammon board open between them. Abbott was a retired Marine sniper with an impressive number of combat kills. Despite her experience in war, she was a laid-back person off duty. She was pretty hot too, which she used to put her enemies at a disadvantage—she didn't look deadly, and by the time people realized she was, it was too late for them. She'd quickly earned the respect of both the Alpha and Omega teams during training exercises and a few missions and cases she'd been involved with so far. While Jake Donovan, the Alpha team's sniper, had been out in San Diego for the past year and a half putting together the Trident Security West Coast team, Lindsey had filled in on both Tampa-based teams.

When they'd been going through the candidates for Omega, Ian and Devon had known they were taking a huge chance on hiring Reese. The former MARSOC— Marine Corps Special Operations Command—Raider had been one of seven Marines taken hostage by insurgents in Iraq thirty months ago. Two of them, Reese and another man, had been the only ones to survive the week as ISIS prisoners of war. The others had been tortured to death, and the remaining two Marines had been scheduled for the same fate before being rescued by a joint MARSOC-SEAL operation. Reese was still dealing with PTSD, but as far as Ian could tell, he had it under control with the help of weekly therapy sessions, which were mandatory for him to remain with Trident. Despite his traumatic experience, he'd already proven he was a kick-ass addition to the team.

Sacked out in another recliner was Valentino "Romeo" Mancini, the pretty-boy of the group. Like many people have said about Jake Donovan over the years, Mancini had "Hollywood" looks. That and his apparent "love 'em and leave 'em" attitude toward women and relationships had led to his moniker. The retired Army SF soldier had come to Trident from the FBI Hostage Rescue Team, bringing his own experience in dealing with certain critical scenarios.

Darius "Batman" Knight had been a known entity to Ian and Dev before joining Trident, having served on SEAL Team Four with the original six-man Alpha Team. After several tours, and dozens of dangerous missions, he'd heard Trident was looking to expand and had immediately put his name in the hat of potential candidates. It had been a no-brainer for him to be offered one of the positions.

Rounding out the team, the final member was Kip "Skipper" Morrison, a retired Army SF and Los Angeles Police Department sniper, who was watching a movie on the TV with Batman. He was originally from the Tampa area and had taken the position with Trident in order to come back and help his family. His parents were divorced, and his father had remarried and had two younger children. When their father and stepmother had been killed in a car accident, Kip and his sister had stepped up to raise their half-siblings, a boy and a girl, ages nine and thirteen, respectively. They were still catching flak from their mother, who'd remained bitter about her divorce after all these years, but Kara, an elementary school teacher, and Kip knew they were doing the right thing raising the orphans. Ian gave them a lot of credit. So far, they were doing a fine job as the children's guardians.

After the months of training, Ian was convinced he and Devon had chosen well and was confident there would be no regrets. Back in Tampa, the new team also had Nathan Cook as their support contact. The uber-geek had been hired from the NSA—National Security Agency—and Trident had needed to get permission from the government to bring the man into the private sector. Thankfully, the contract they'd all signed enabled Cook to still log into the NSA's mainframe for research, since most of Trident's missions were the result of government contracts.

Once they landed at a small airport outside Montrose, Colorado, they'd drive into the mountains to a small town named Ouray. Then tomorrow, the team would board a Blackhawk helicopter with Babs at the controls. It'd been easier to contract out a local, private aircraft instead of flying their own bird from Florida to Colorado. The flight company's pilot had agreed to ride shotgun as Ian had wanted his entire staff working as they would in the field. The team would fast rope into the mountains with a two-day hike out. Provisions would be minimal, ensuring they worked together for survival. They would have a satellite radio, which was only to be used in life-or-death situations—a broken leg wouldn't qualify. With their combined experience, they'd easily be able to get their injured party back to the extraction point.

Movement from the two rows of first-class-style seating at the front of the jet caught Ian's eye. A pair of arms stretched over the back of the seat, and he smiled. His wife/submissive Angie had woken from her nap. He took a step forward then stopped and glanced down at the coffee in his hand. Grimacing, he sighed, took a final mouthful of the delicious brew, and poured the rest down the sink.

Bab's stared at him, horrified. "That's a sacrilege."

"I agree, but the smell of coffee is one of the things that turns Angie green at the moment. Until her morning sickness passes, I can't bring it within ten feet of her."

Chuckling, she toasted him with her mug. "And you called me a saint."

He opened the galley's refrigerator and grabbed a bottle of Coke and another of ginger ale. Striding through the cabin, his stomach growled—if he was hungry, then Angie must be starving. He never thought there would come a day when she would out-eat him, but when she wasn't sick to her stomach, she was filling it, which was fine with him. What wasn't fine was that some of her food cravings made his own stomach sour. Pickles and ice cream had nothing on his wife's choices these days.

"Nice to see you awake, Angel." He held out the bottle of ginger ale to her. "Did you sleep well?"

Her face lit up when she saw him, and she patted the seat next to her, before taking the soda from him. He felt a stirring in his groin as he sat. Fifty years from now, when they were old and gray, she'd still be beautiful and make him want her. "Thank you, and yes, I did. Where are we?"

"About an hour from the airport. Do you want something to eat?"

Before she had a chance to answer, her stomach did it for her by rumbling. Ian smiled and placed his hand on the small swell of her abdomen. He couldn't wait to see her belly grow with their child because she really wasn't showing yet. But her breasts had already grown larger and more sensitive, which he loved.

"What's on the menu?"

"I had food services stock a few of your favorite, weird cravings."

Her smile grew, and he knew he was about to cringe at whatever she said next. "Bacon and Hershey's syrup?"

Yup, talk about a sacrilege. "No, but I can make you mayonnaise on cinnamon raisin bread, peanut butter and baloney on rye, or there's vanilla ice cream and honey barbecue chips." She loved to mix them together, and Ian couldn't stand to watch her eat it—or any of the other weird combinations of food for that matter.

"A mayo sandwich, please. And a Yoo-hoo, if there is some."

Rolling his eyes, he stood. "I hope Jordyn craves that if Carter ever gets her pregnant." Their friend, who was a US spy, hated even looking at mayo for some reason.

Heading back to the galley, Ian knew no matter what his Angel wanted, he'd get it for her—even if it was something physically impossible, like the moon. However, that didn't mean he wasn't going to gag in the process.

Chapter Two

Sitting down on her bed in the room she was sharing with Lindsey at a small B & B, Babs doffed her prosthesis, the socket it was attached to, and the gel sleeve protecting her tear-drop-shaped residual limb. She'd recently had a new socket custom made by a talented prosthetist Ian had found for her in Tampa. It fit much better than her old one had, since the shape of her stump had changed over time, which was expected. The prosthetist had scanned what was left of her lower leg with a laser to give it the best fit possible. Despite the titanium prosthesis weighing much less than her original leg had, her residual limb felt so much lighter without it on. The tricks her body played on her mind about the missing leg still messed with her. The phantom pain and tingling she felt in her non-existent toes flared a few times a day.

Even though the temperature in the room was set at seventy degrees, the air still felt chilly against the sensitive skin which stretched over the tapered stump, and prickling goosebumps arose all the way up to her hip.

She'd shared rooms before with the female Trident operative and was now comfortable in the shorts and tank she normally wore to bed while in the woman's presence. During their first time sharing a room, Lindsey had explained that a childhood friend had lost an arm at the shoulder during a boating accident, and she was all too familiar with amputees. She'd jokingly said she was more repulsed by Babs's Air Force tattoo on her back than she'd ever be about the stump—once a jarhead, always a jarhead.

While her roommate was listening to a book on her Kindle with headphones, as she cleaned her sniper rifle, Babs used her crutches to move into the bathroom to clean her leg. She sat on the toilet lid and wet a washcloth, then added soap. Gently cleaning the delicate skin, she inspected it for any signs of developing sores, blisters, or rashes.

Like most amputees, it had taken her a while to accept her loss and mentally and physically recover. But while she had, her ex-husband, Eddie Quinn, had never gotten over the fact she was "damaged," and it had led to their divorce. She couldn't stand the pity and regret she saw every time she caught him staring at what was left of her leg. Losing her high school sweetheart, six months after her accident, had sucked the spirit out of her more than the loss of her leg had. But she'd overcome both and was determined to move on without him—if only she could stop dreaming about him. While her mind hated him, her body still responded when he showed up in her nighttime fantasies. It had been more than three years since her final tour of duty had begun, and the last time the man had made love to her, and yet her body hadn't forgotten at all.

There had been many a night where she'd woken up on the precipice of an orgasm because he'd been doing wild and wicked things to her in her dreams. But once reality kicked in, she would grieve the destruction of her marriage all over again.

She thought back to last night's memory which was still quite vivid in her mind.

The sound of the back door opening and closing had me alert in an instant, but I eased back down on the bed as I heard Eddie performing his coming-home-after-work ritual. His keys clinked when they were dropped into a bowl on the kitchen counter. His boots thumped softly on the floor as he toed them off, leaving them by the back door. She knew he'd start unbuttoning his Sheriff's Department uniform shirt as he strode down the hallway to their bedroom. When the door swung open, my gaze met his. From his calm, relaxed expression, I could tell he'd had a nice, quiet shift for a change.

"I'm surprised you're still awake, Tempe," he said as he removed his shirt and threw it into a laundry hamper next to the closet. "I didn't wake you, did I?"

I stretched my arms and legs like a seductive kitten. "Mmm, my body is always awake when you're near, my love."

Putting his sidearm in the drawer of his nightstand, he gave me a salacious grin. "Is that right? I think you need to show me."

I bit my bottom lip as I slowly pulled my tank top up my torso and over my head, tossing it on the floor. I then lifted my hips and got rid of my cotton sleep shorts—I wouldn't be wearing them for the rest of the night. When Eddie was in bed with me, I always slept naked, but on nights when he was working, I would don a pair of shorts and a tank, which is what I usually slept in on my tours of duty.

Stripping off the rest of his clothes, Eddie climbed into bed and crawled over to my side. He was already hard. Even after being together for ten years, six of them while married, we were still hot for each other. It only took a glance, a wink, a suggestive comment, or a lick of one's lips, and we were both ready to fuck like rabbits.

Laying on his side next to me, Eddie ran his hand up my thigh to the junction between my legs, causing thousands of goosebumps to pebble on my skin. His fingers found me already wet and waiting for him. He lightly caressed my folds before flicking my clit— my hips bouncing off the bed.

"Stop teasing me," I moaned. "I want fast and furious tonight."

His mouth closed around one of my nipples, and he sucked and licked it, driving me mad as he always did. Some of my friends complained that sex bored them, or it took a lot to get them in the mood. Not me. Eddie knew how to make me beg, and my body sing. While we had both been virgins the first time, we'd made love in our teens, and had only been with each other since, we were open-minded and loved to explore the internet, learning new ways to please each other.

Eddie's fingers dropped lower again, and curled into my sex, parting my folds and entering me. Despite my begging and undulating hips, he set about fucking me with two fingers at a torturously slow pace. One of my hands went to his short, black hair and held him to my breast, while the other scratched up his back the way I knew he liked. His hand left my pussy for a moment, and he spread my legs further apart, settling one of his own legs between them to keep them that way. Letting go of my nipple, he kissed his way over to the other one and attacked my pussy again.

I gasped for breath as the need to come coursed through me. "Faster! Eddie, please, faster!"

"Mm-mm. Not yet, baby. I want to feast on you first." Stopping everything, and going up on his knees, he grabbed a pillow and placed it under my hips when I lifted them for him. Moving between my legs, he put his hands on the backs of my thighs and pushed them toward my chest, exposing me for his viewing pleasure. When I was OCONUS, it was hard to keep myself shaven, but it was one of the first things I took care of upon returning to the US. We both loved how sensitive I was while bare.

Lowering his head, he took a long, luxurious lick up my pussy, then his hazel eyes lifted to meet my dreamy gaze. "Mmm, there's my dessert. Mine and only mine. I've been looking forward to it all day. Sweet and spicy." He tasted me again and again, then added a finger to rub my clit in time to his ministrations.

I moaned and writhed under his talented tongue and fingers. He switched things up and put his mouth on my clit and sucked while he began to finger fuck me again. With every thrust, I climbed higher and higher. "Please! I want you with me!"

With a wicked grin, he crawled up my body and took my mouth with his. My taste on his tongue and lips was one of the most erotic things about sex with my husband. Eddie lined his cock up with my slit and began to ease into me.

Several loud knocks startled Babs, and she came back to the present. Her hand was down her shorts, and she yanked it out as Lindsey's voice came through the closed bathroom door. "Babs, you almost done? I need to use the toilet."

"Uh . . . um . . . yeah. Just give me a minute, and it's all yours."

"No problem."

Turning the water back on, she washed and dried her hands. After making sure her residual limb was dry, she used her crutches to stand and stared into the mirror. The desire that had probably been in her gaze moments before had been replaced by regret and anger. Hopefully one of these days, sooner rather than later, Eddie Quinn would be barely a memory. Maybe then she'd be able to find someone who looked at her like she was a whole woman.

Hoisting his pack over his shoulder at 0800 hours, Kip Morrison took a final glance around the motel room he'd shared with Romeo, making sure neither of them were leaving anything behind. While Ian, Angie, Babs, and Costello had stayed in a B&B up the road, the rest of them had bunked in this small motel, due to lack of enough available rooms in both places. Kip was surprised they had five rooms between the two businesses to begin with. They were in the middle of bum-fuck Colorado, and there wasn't much in the way of lodging or entertainment in the area.

Both men were dressed in camouflage tactical clothing and had various weapons strapped to their bodies, as if this were a real mission. The team had been training for months, while being used for various missions and cases whenever possible, paired up with members of the TS Alpha team.

As Romeo opened the door leading to the parking lot, Kip's cell phone rang. Pulling it out of his pocket, he checked the screen. His teammate glanced over his shoulder, and Kip waved him on. "Tell Ian I'll be out in a minute."

"No prob, Skipper." The door clicked shut.

Sitting back on the bed he'd slept in, Kip answered the call. "Hey, sis. Everything okay?"

"Yeah, I just wanted to ask you something before you go silent." Between his military tours, SWAT detail, and now his job with Trident, his sister was used to him being unavailable for hours or days at a time. "Are you sure you're going to be home by Saturday?"

"Unless something happens on the mountain, we'll be home Friday afternoon, maybe early evening. Why?"

"Shane's got a makeup swim meet on Saturday at ten o'clock, and Rach has softball tryouts at the same time."

Their half brother and sister had become Kip and Kara's world these past eighteen months. Kara's phone call, letting him know of their father and stepmother's fatal accident, had come on the same day he'd learned Trident Security in Tampa was looking for candidates for their new team. Finding out about the job had been a fluke. A friend of one of Kip's SWAT teammates had been talking about it after work—the guy had applied for a position, hoping to get into the more lucrative paying private sector. Two days after the funeral in St. Petersburg, Kip had met with Ian and Devon Sawyer and thrown his hat into the ring.

While he'd loved his job with LAPD, thanks to a drunk driver, who'd also been killed, he was now a father, figuratively speaking, at the age of thirty two. Instead of uprooting Rachelle, Shane, and Kara, and moving them to California, it had been much easier on all of them for him to return to his hometown. As soon as the Sawyer brothers had told him he was hired, he'd given his supervisors and team notice of his resignation, packed up his belongings, and headed east.

The opportunity had not only given him a new career, it had also been the last straw in his already rocky marriage. He'd met Monica when he'd been a rookie on the police force. She'd been gorgeous, sexy, and fun—everyone said they were the perfect couple—and after a whirlwind romance, they'd gotten married eight months later. It'd been on their honeymoon in Hawaii when Kip realized he'd made a big mistake. They'd been in lust, not truly in love, and had gotten caught up in the whole idea of being happily married following a huge wedding. He'd spent four years trying to make it work, but then she'd cheated on him, and in spite, he'd cheated on her—something he wasn't proud of. The last few months, leading up to Kara's tear-filled phone call, he and Monica had been more like roommates who did nothing but bitch at each other. The divorce had been final ten months ago, and Kip doubted he'd ever talk to the woman again. Last he'd heard, she was already on her way to marrying husband number two. Kip wished the poor guy luck.

"Hey, Kip—you still there?"

He shook his head, vanquishing the memories that had led him to this point in his life. "Yeah, I'm here. Sorry. Zoned out for a moment. I'll take Shane to the meet. I'll ask Boss-man to have Colleen put it on the calendar." His new employers and Trident's very efficient officer manager had been great, letting him work around the kids' schedules when the caseload allowed it. Even though it was a Saturday, that didn't mean Kip would be off. Details were always popping up and needing to be filled.

"Okay. Um . . . there's one other thing." Kara sounded worried, and Kip's shoulders tensed. "No, never mind, I've got to finish getting ready for work. We'll talk when you get home."

Glancing at his watch, he knew he had to get his ass outside before someone from the team came pounding on the door, but he still asked, "Sis, what is it? Tell me."

A loud sigh came over the line. "I think Rachelle's being bullied at school."

"Rach? I thought she had a lot of girlfriends at school."

"I'm not sure it's girls who are bullying her. I think it's some of the pubescent, horny-as-shit boys. I overheard her on the phone last night talking to her friend Trisha, but when I asked her about it, she blew me off and yelled at me for eavesdropping. Tell me I wasn't like that when I was her age."

Kip snorted. "If I did, I'd be lying." A knock on the door told him his time was up. "Listen, I gotta run. I'll see if Rach will talk to me about it when I get home." His little sister and brother had bonded with him ever since they were toddlers, despite the miles between them. He'd made a point to call and Skype them as much as possible, and that diligence had been a blessing when it had fallen to him to be a positive, male role model.

"All right. Be safe. Don't get eaten by a bear—I need help raising these two."

Chuckling, he said goodbye, then stood and headed for the door. The entire team, plus the boss and his wife, were gathered around the two vans they'd rented. Babs would be driving one to the small, private airport where the helicopter was waiting for them, while Ian drove the other. After dumping the team in the fucking middle of nowhere, the two would come back to Ouray and wait for the team to haul ass out of the wilderness.

As he strode toward the group, his thoughts flickered to Rachelle. At thirteen, she was a pretty girl with long, blonde hair and classic facial features. Watching her grow up, he'd known there'd come a day he'd be beating the boys off her with a stick. It looked like that day had come. While his sister had said Rach was getting bullied, Kip wondered if the reason behind it was the boys thought she was hot and didn't know how to deal with their raging hormones yet. Then again, he could be wrong—it'd been a long time since he'd gone through puberty.

"What's the matter?" Ian arched an eyebrow at Kip, and the others turned to stare at him. Obviously, his concern about his little sister had been written across his face.

He waved a hand to reassure everyone it wasn't anything big. They'd all met Kara, Shane, and Rachelle over the past few months, so he didn't mind sharing his worries with his team and boss. "Nothing I can take care of from here. Kara thinks Rach is being bullied by some boys at school. Not sure if it's because they like her or if they're really being assholes. I'm going to have to start showing her how to defend herself in case any of the little shits get too touchy-feely."

Ian opened up his mouth to say something, but Angie was quicker. "She can come to the self-defense class Lindsey and Charlotte are teaching the subs."

Having been busy on a few details lately, which had kept him away from the Trident offices more often than not, Kip had no idea what the boss's wife was talking about. Ian saw his confusion. "As I was about to say, before my Angel beat me to it, if you want, Costello and Charlotte are giving lessons to some of The Covenant's subs. Jenn and Alyssa have been helping out, and a few subs signed up with friends not in the lifestyle, so it's a vanilla group. Rach is welcome to come as long as it's all right with Costello and Charlotte."

Jenn Mullins was Ian's twenty-one-year-old goddaughter, while Alyssa Wagner was a teen who was the charge of Alpha Team member Ben "Boomer" Michaelson's parents after she'd become an orphan about eighteen months ago. The Michalesons, along with Alyssa, had moved from Sarasota to Tampa last month to be closer to Boomer and his new wife, Kat. Charlotte—aka Mistress China—was a Domme at the BDSM club, as well as a probation officer, who knew how to kick some serious criminal ass, from what he'd heard. Kip had met her several times at get-togethers at the Trident compound. She was gorgeous, petite, and exotic looking, and probably had the ex-cons shaking in their shoes if need be.

Now, he vaguely remembered hearing about the class the two women were teaching, since submissive females were being targeted, tortured, and killed. He knew several cops he'd worked with were in the lifestyle, and if he were being honest, what little of it he'd learned over the years intrigued him. But Monica had turned her nose up at the idea of trying it the few times he'd mentioned it, and since he'd moved back to Florida, work and the kids had taken up most of his time. One of these days, he'd check out the club.

The Omega teammates had all been cleared to enter The Covenant while it was open, and each operative had signed a non-disclosure contract, whether they intended to play or not. The contract had been mandatory at their time of hire—the Sawyer brothers needed to ensure the club members' privacy, and since it was on Trident property, there were plenty of times Kip and the others saw club members coming and going. He knew Foster was a longtime practicing Dom, and McCabe was an apprenticing Dom at the club, having gotten into the lifestyle after signing on with TS Omega.

Dressed in camouflage tactical gear like the rest of the team, Lindsey nodded at Kip. "It's fine with me, and I doubt Charlotte will have a problem with it either. Rach can even bring a friend or two if she wants, so she doesn't feel like the only kid. We meet in the compound's gym on Mondays and Wednesdays."

"Sounds good," Kip responded. "I'll talk to her about it when we get home. Thanks."

Ian clapped his hands together. "All right. Is that it? Any other family problems we need to deal with before I throw your asses out of the helo?" Behind her husband's back, Angie rolled her eyes. "Yes? No? Good. Load the fuck up!"

CHAPTER THREE

After saying goodbye to Angie, who wasn't feeling well enough to take a chopper ride, McCabe climbed into the back seat of one of the vans and snorted at his co-leader who took the front passenger seat next to Babs. "Foster, man, we really have to get you some different shades."

The two men had been the first of Omega Team hired by Trident eighteen months ago. They worked so well together that the Sawyer brothers decided to use it to their advantage, making them co-leaders. The two men had fallen into an easy friendship from the start and respected each other's opinions and experience.

Right now, the man was looking over his shoulder, his eyebrows bunched up behind his Oakleys before he took the sunglasses off and inspected them. Like the rest of the men on the team, he hadn't shaved in about two weeks, wanting the extra protection against the cold they'd be feeling at nightfall in the mountains. They would be encountering snow at the higher elevations before moving into areas that would be half white and the other green thanks to the milder winter. "What's wrong with them?"

"First of all, shouldn't you be wearing Foster Grants, for the name alone? And secondly, no matter how scruffy your face is, those things still scream 'Secret Service.'"

On the seat beside him, Knight and Mancini laughed. Even Babs chuckled and said, "Looks like you finally got your nickname, Foster. Your team will have to vote on it, but I love the tag 'Shades.'" Not having a military background, Cain hadn't had a nickname, and his teammates had been waiting for one to make itself known.

Romeo slapped the former agent's shoulder. "That's it! About fucking time, too."

Shoving the glasses back on his face, Foster gave them the finger. "Fuck you all. And no, there's no relation between me and Foster Grants. If there were, I'd be fucking rich."

The usual team camaraderie and ball-busting continued for the rest of the drive. Pulling into the small airport, Babs followed Ian's van to the second hangar on the left. On a nearby helipad sat a dark Sikorsky UH-60 Blackhawk Medium-Lift Transport. It looked so out of place among the mostly white, blue, and red Cessna airplanes and two civilian Bell helicopters. A tall, darkskinned man wearing a flight jumpsuit exited the hangar and strode toward Ian as he climbed out of the van. While Babs went to join them to be introduced to the other pilot, the Omega team poured from the two vehicles, gathering up their deployment bags and equipment.

Lindsey gave Foster a little hip check. "Ready for your first real fast-roping, stud?"

The man had practiced with Devon Sawyer and Marco DeAngelis of the Alpha Team many times doing some rope ascents and descents from the company's training building, some cliffs, and Trident's own helicopter. It wasn't as if the Secret Service did a lot of rock climbing or jumped out of perfectly good choppers, and this would be his first rapid deployment as if it were a real mission. The highest fast-roping he'd done so far had been from approximately seventy-five feet—this one would be about fifty feet higher. At thirty-four feet, a person loses their depth perception. If they are going to have issues with heights or vertigo, that's where they'd have it. Foster had passed all that with flying colors.

"As long as Batman goes first and breaks my fall."

The retired SEAL grinned. "I'll make sure my foot is in the air, so it goes up your ass."

"Unless he goes possum," Tristan joked. A "possum rappeller" is when a person inadvertently gets turned upside down from not holding their brake hand, or the hand lowest on the rope, tight enough. It's then up to the rappel master, in this case, Ian, to pull on the rope in such a way to get them upright again. "Then just make sure Shades opens his mouth wide enough, so you don't kick out his teeth."

As Babs and the other pilot went through the checklist to make sure the bird was safe to fly, the team and Ian loaded the gear into the passenger area. Once they were done and had a few more minutes before takeoff, Ian pulled a camera out of the side pocket of his tan, cargo pants. "Angie wants a picture of the team, so she can sketch it for the office."

Tristan had been impressed with the woman's talent.

There was a large, framed sketch of the Alpha Team now hanging in the reception area, and he assumed this one would be put next to it. Standing on the left side of the helicopter, the team closed ranks, and Tristan put an arm around Foster's shoulders and the other over Mancini's.

"Don't fucking smile."

Of course, the boss's growled order had everyone laughing, as he probably intended. He took several shots before putting the camera away again as the team pulled on their safety belts, harnesses, and tethers needed for the fast-roping.

Once she was done with the checklist, Babs glanced over her shoulder at the team. "Load up, boys and girls. It's time to get this show in the clouds. I hope everyone had a light breakfast."

Tristan chuckled as he took a seat, secured a belt over his hips, and put on his headphones. The female pilot was known for taking them on roller coaster rides hundreds of feet in the air. Most of the team had tossed their cookies in a barf bag during a training flight at one time or another.

As everyone strapped in, the rotors of the helicopter began to spin faster and faster. Like she was performing a levitation act, Babs pulled back on the control stick and lifted them into the air with nary a hiccup.

Despite her warning, Babs gave them a smooth flight to their drop-off point about fifteen minutes away by air. The team pulled on their heat-resistant gloves, which would protect their hands during the fast descent on the rope. Their flight helmets with visors, would protect their heads and eyes. During the air time, the team attached the rappel ropes to the steel, donut rings bolted to the floor of the chopper and the opposite ends to their deployment bags which held everything they were taking with them.

As Babs hovered 125 feet above a small clearing below the rock face of Dallas Peak, west of Ouray, everyone in the back stood and removed their headphones. Widening his stance for balance, Ian turned to McCabe and double-checked the man's harness and anchor point connection—he would be the first one out the door. Moments after he pushed off and dropped, Romeo would be the first one descending on the second rope.

From here on out, they'd be working with hand signals due to the volume of the rotors. Once confirming McCabe was ready, Ian gestured for him to throw his and two other deployment bags attached to the same rope out the door, far enough out to avoid them going between the chopper and its skid. After his cleared and dropped, Batman threw a second rope/bag combo out the door. There were two reasons for sending the bags down first—one less thing the team had to deal with during the drop, and the weight helped stabilize the rope. Ian stuck his head out the door and looked down, making sure the bags were touching the ground and the rope was free of knots.

With the next hand signal, McCabe sat on the floor, swung his legs out of the bird, and set the balls of his feet on the skid. Holding the rope, he pivoted 180 degrees and faced Ian and the rest of the team. His feet were shoulder-width apart, his knees locked, the rope was between his legs, and his body was bent at the waist toward the helicopter. His upper, guide hand had a light grip on the rope, while his brake hand was tighter around the rope at the small of his back.

There were two ways to fast-rope down, and it

depended on how far off the ground they were. At a much lower altitude, they could forego the harness and just use their hands and feet as their guides and brakes. However, from this height, they'd use a seat harness and their hands only—using their boot-covered feet could damage the rope at the speed they'd be dropping at.

When Ian gave the "go" signal, McCabe flexed his knees and pushed over the skid, allowing the rope to pass through his hands. The eight-feet-per-second descent was smooth with no jerky stops. About halfway down, he started the brake process and felt the weight of Abbott starting her descent on the rope high above him. When his feet hit the ground, about a mile above the tree line elevation, he cleared his rappel ring from the rope, as Romeo landed a few feet away, then stepped out of the way of his teammates. Their female sniper was the next one with boots on the ground. One by one, alternating on the two lines, they landed. When they were all clear and unhooked, Ian dropped his end of the ropes down to them. Tilting his head back, McCabe gave their boss a thumbs up then watched as the helicopter gained altitude and headed back to the airport. From the time he'd stepped out onto the skid until all boots were on the ground, less than ninety seconds had passed.

As Mancini, Morrison, and Reese wound the ropes up, the others untied the deployment bags. Once everyone had loaded the gear on their backs, McCabe checked his compass, then led his team to the east. They had plenty of miles on the rough terrain to cover over the next several hours before they could take a break for lunch. After that, it would be a repeat of the morning.

Since joining Trident, McCabe had done quite a few

missions in several parts of the world and in different climates, but it had been a while since he'd been up in the mountains. It didn't take long for him, and the others, to note the lower oxygen levels in the higher altitudes, and he adjusted his pace so they wouldn't be gasping for air anytime soon. It was going to be a long two days at any rate.

Thank God I live for this shit.

Holding the door open, Ian allowed Babs and CC, who'd joined them upon their return, to enter the little diner before he followed them in. He saw Angie waving them over to where she sat at a table for four at the back of the establishment. He was glad to see the color had returned to her face—she'd been so pale that morning. When they'd landed the helicopter at the airport, he'd called to see how she was doing and had gotten the response he'd been hoping for—she was hungry and would meet them for a late breakfast. Her day had started in the bathroom with some dry heaves, followed by some very bland crackers, so the fact she had her appetite back made him feel better. He hoped her morning sickness would soon be a thing of the past. As her husband and Dom, he hated to see her ill or miserable for any reason—especially since getting her pregnant had caused it.

Instead of joining the couple, Babs and CC veered off and took seats at the counter, telling Ian to enjoy a quiet meal with his wife. While it may have seemed like a kind gesture, the boss knew it was because they were both coffee addicts who didn't want Angie getting sick to her stomach again. And God forbid they gave up their caffeine fixes for an hour or so.

Angie didn't miss their actions either. "They don't want me throwing up all over the place, *huh?*" she asked as Ian sat across from her, with his back against the far wall of the diner, as was his custom. Like the rest of the Trident operatives, he hated having his back to the rest of a room, needing to constantly assess his surroundings no matter how mundane and harmless they might seem.

Not answering the rhetorical question, Ian smiled. "Have I told you how beautiful you are today?"

"No. But you have told me that my breasts look even bigger."

He chuckled. "Well, they do. It's a shame they're too sensitive for clamps. I'll have to come up with something else to torture you with until you beg me to fuck you silly." Her eyes widened as she glanced around to see if anyone had overheard him, which he knew no one had. He gently took her hand, and her gaze returned to him and softened. "Since I've been remiss, let me state that you are beautiful, stunning, gorgeous, exquisite . . ." The corners of her mouth climbed upward, revealing two small dimples. ". . . and downright adorable, and I'm very close to saying to hell with breakfast, so I can take you back to bed."

Her grin turned seductive, and his dick twitched. "*Mmm.* While any other time I might be okay with that, Little Bit will not be happy, I can assure you. He or she is hungry, which makes mommy hungry too."

"How about we feed Little Bit first, then go back to our room so Master Daddy can have his feast."

A blush stole across her face, but before she could give

him a verbal answer, their gray-haired waitress ambled over. As Angie ordered enough food for sextuplets, Ian perused the menu quickly, before adding his choice to the list the older woman was jotting down.

Handing the menus back to the waitress, he noticed the local sheriff was standing by the counter next to Babs and CC, talking with the diner's owner. Ian had met the lawman on several occasions when SEAL Team Four, and then the Trident Alpha Team, had come to the area to do the same training run Omega was doing at the moment. But Sheriff Wayne Collins didn't appear to be his normally spit-shined self today. He was a retired Marine, and Ian had never seen him so disheveled.

Worried something was wrong, Ian was about to stand when, not surprisingly, Babs turned and gestured for him to join them after evidently hearing something which caused her concern.

"I'll be right back, Angel."

Ian had called and left a courtesy message this morning with the sheriff's dispatcher as a reminder that he and his team were in town for a training run. It was always a good idea to let the local law know when they had trained men and women with military-grade weapons running around the area. All Ian had been told was that the man hadn't been available to speak to him at the time, but the message would be passed on.

Striding over, he got a better look at the fifty-year-old man. His eyes were bloodshot, and Ian's uneasiness increased. Collins sensed a newcomer approaching, and when he turned, his eyes flashed with recognition.

Ian held out his hand. "Sheriff, if you don't mind me saying so, you look like shit. What's up?"

After shaking his hand, Collins went back to putting his uniform hat in a death grip. "Hey, Sawyer. Forgot your team was coming up this week, but now that you're here, I could use your help. Did they get dropped in the usual spot?" When Ian nodded, the man continued. "My niece, Mallory, went hiking yesterday near Lower Blue Lake, and didn't come home. Her father's a buddy of mine from the Corps, who ended up falling in love with my sister, and he's made sure Mallory knows how to handle herself out there. Her car's still parked at the lookout she usually goes to. She's an amateur photographer and sells her photos on some of those online stock sites. Every week, she goes out once or twice, and always takes a backpack with food, water, satellite phone, and bear spray, in case she runs into trouble."

"Any sign of her?"

"No. Not her backpack, camera, or anything else. It's like she disappeared off the side of the mountain. We've got people searching, but the initial K9s I brought in last night, before it got too dark, lost her scent about two miles down the trail she took. I'm just heading back to the search area after crashing for a few hours. We've also got a storm watch for tomorrow. There's a possibility a cold weather front, south of here, might take a left turn. If that happens, we're looking at about a foot of snow in some areas." And a drastic reduction in the chances of finding the girl alive.

"I can go back to the airport and see if there's a bird I can take up to help search," Babs volunteered.

"I'll go with you as an extra set of eyes," CC added.

After getting the approval from Collins, Ian nodded at his employees. "Do it."

The sheriff rattled off a description of the young woman, and what they thought she'd been wearing, to Babs as CC got their breakfasts to go. Ian pivoted to face Angie and held up two fingers before pulling out his cell. He dialed the satellite phone Knight was carrying and waited for it to be answered.

It took four rings. "Miss us already, Boss-man."

"You wish. Listen, we've got a hiker missing since yesterday afternoon." He gave them her description. "Keep an eye out for her—we've got no idea which way she was headed or how far she got. I doubt she's anywhere near you at the moment, but you may cross paths as you work your way back here. When I get search coordinates and a better idea of what's going on, I'll call you back."

"Sounds good."

Disconnecting the call, Ian told the sheriff he'd be right back, then headed toward Angie to tell her their plans had changed, so he could go help with the search. So much for his afternoon feast.

Chapter Four

The morning sun peeking through the trees hit Mallory directly in the face, waking her. She blinked several times and took in her surroundings. The cold from the air and ground penetrated her jeans and lightweight sweater and jacket, causing her to shiver. A small campfire that had given her some warmth had died out at some point over the past two or three hours. Her arms and legs were stiff as hell, and she tried to stretch the kinks out of them.

Her hands were still restrained in front of her, and she was lying right where she'd been since late last night—in some sort of mountain camp, God knew where. It was at least a two-hour hike at a decent clip from where she'd been taking photos yesterday. In addition to the two men who'd kidnapped her, two others had walked into the camp long after the sun had gone down. From what she could tell, they were related—three brothers, and the older man was their father. He'd been none too pleased with the two who'd brought her into the camp, and there'd been a lot of yelling and a few unanswered punches thrown by the patriarch of the family.

When everything had died back down, she'd hoped they'd release her, but instead they'd taken turns standing guard so she couldn't escape. A rope had been tied around her waist with the other end wrapped around a tree. Mallory had no idea what was in store for her, but she'd continue to do what she'd done ever since the men had grabbed her. She'd bide her time and wait for an opportunity to escape, then run like hell. The problem was she'd been so scared as they'd marched her through the woods for several miles, far from the main trails, that she was having trouble pinpointing where they were. All she knew was they'd headed east and then southeast based on where the sun had set.

If it wasn't four to one, she'd have a much better chance of escaping. Running through the woods wouldn't be a problem for her with her cross country track team history. Her father and uncle had taught her many things over the years about what to do if attacked or kidnapped, such as how to escape from a car's trunk, pick a set of handcuffs while wearing them, or snap a zip tie restraining her wrists. Who knew that last one would finally be put to the test? She just had to wait for the right moment.

Out here in the wilderness, though, she had other things to worry about if she did manage to escape. Bears, mountain lions, lack of food, water, and warm clothing, and other hazards topped the list.

A thumping noise began to pulsate through the trees,

and it took her a moment to realize it was an approaching helicopter. Could it be a search team out looking for her? Her family had to know she was missing and had undoubtedly contacted Uncle Wayne at the Sheriff's Department.

As the helicopter's rotors cutting through the air got louder and louder, Mallory's head whipped around. The trees were too tall and dense in this area, and there was no way she'd be spotted unless there was a clearing she could run to. As if knowing her intent, the burly man with the facial scar who'd first confronted her—his father had called him Jessup, as well as a fucking asshole, which she agreed with—moved closer and leered at her. "Don't get any ideas, missy. There's no way they'll be able to see you from up there."

Her heart sank as she realized he was right, and the helicopter move further west at a decent clip.

"Why won't you let me go?" It was a question she'd asked numerous times over the past fifteen hours or so, with no answer. For some reason, the four men looked familiar, but she didn't know why, and honestly, at the moment, she didn't care. They obviously knew how to survive out here.

"Because you seen us," responded the brother who had been in the camp with his father when she'd arrived. He was eating what looked like beef jerky out of a pouch, and Mallory's stomach growled in hunger. This one seemed much younger than the other two, and not as threatening. In fact, he appeared almost shy. Maybe she could convince him to let her go if the others weren't around.

"Shut up, Billy Ray," the father growled as he stepped

back into the camp. The way he was adjusting his pants, Mallory figured he'd just peed. And that made her own need to go register in her mind. "Darrell, give me her bag. Let's see what the little girlie has in there."

The third brother passed her backpack to his father who opened it and shuffled through it. She hoped he would give her one of the bottles of water and a granola bar, but first things first. "I have to pee." The older man glared at her as she struggled to stand. "Look, I don't know what you want from me, but if I don't get two seconds of privacy, I'm going to pee my pants. As unpleasant as that sounds, it's the truth."

The same statement had worked last night with Darrell and Jessup, and thankfully, it worked again this morning. The father continued to dig through her things. "Billy Ray, take her behind that rock over there."

"Yes, Pa."

As the other men ate and gathered up their belongings, Billy Ray untied the rope at her waist and led her to where his father had indicated. A blush stole over his cheeks. "I won't watch, but don't try to get away. Pa will be mad." True to his word, he turned his back to her, but still stood only a few feet away.

She felt a little relief since his brothers hadn't given her the same courtesy yesterday. She'd used her coat to cover herself as best she could then. Undoing her snap and zipper with her restrained hands, she used the large rock for support as she pushed her jeans lower. Once she squatted, it took her a few moments to finally relax enough to urinate. Within minutes, she was decent once more.

When he heard her moving around, Billy Ray asked if

it was okay if he turned around. Despite being held hostage by him and his family, Mallory found his question endearing. "Yes. Thank you."

She gave him a small smile when he faced her, and his cheeks turned pink again. Yes, he was the weakest link, and if she was going to make it out of this alive, he was the one she'd have to win over. With the others, she didn't have a chance.

Billy Ray escorted her back to the makeshift camp. The contents of her backpack were spread out on the ground. While her car keys were there, she'd left her wallet in the glove compartment of her Toyota, so the men still thought her name was Susan. The SIM card had been removed from her camera and broken in half, and her satellite phone had been impaled by her hunting knife. Her bear spray had been taken from her yesterday and was currently hanging from a belt loop of Darrell's camo pants. The older man pocketed her compass then began to put everything else back in her bag.

Mallory wondered if he'd give her water and food. There was only one way to find out. "Can I have one of the waters and the granola bars? If we're going to be walking again, I need them for energy, otherwise, I'll slow you down." She didn't give a crap about that, but she would need to keep her strength up to escape when a chance arose.

A faint thumping resounded overhead again, getting louder every second. The helicopter zoomed past them, and Mallory's heart sank. If they were searching for her, they wouldn't have been going that fast. But it was enough to worry her captors.

The father stood and shoved one of the waters and a

granola bar in her hands. "Eat it on the way. Let's move out."

"Shit," Jessup muttered while glaring at Mallory. A chill went down her spine. "You better be a good fuck and worth the wait, bitch."

Oh God. Now she knew what her fate would be if she didn't escape. Opening the granola bar, she quickly ate it, even though her taste buds thought it was sawdust. Guzzling half the water, she hydrated her body to prepare it for the run of her life, because if it failed, she would suffer until these men finally killed her.

Leaning against a tree, Lindsey Abbott chewed the apple cinnamon bar she was having for dessert after an MRE lunch. She'd gotten used to the ready-to-eat meals during her time in the Marines, but after dining on civilian food for the past year, the three-cheese-tortellini, that'd been her favorite of the disgusting meals, tasted a lot worse than she remembered. At least, it came with a pack of M&Ms she'd save for later. They'd been hiking for four hours with a fifteen minute break at the two hour mark and had another four to five hours to go before they reached the spot Ian had mapped out for them. It was a rock outcropping where they'd have some shelter from the elements for the night.

The rest of the team was scattered around her, finishing off their own meals, and she made a mental note to stay far away from Foster after seeing he'd ended up with a chicken burrito bowl. It was almost a surefire bet that in a few hours his digestive system would be revolting against the meal. From the sly smirks the rest of the team was sending his way, they surmised the same thing. Being former military at times like this was definitely an advantage.

A few conversations combined with the sounds of nature, but Lindsey closed her eyes and rested her head against the tree, ignoring how strands from her brown ponytail caught on the bark. Her thoughts were miles away, back in Tampa, with the man she'd almost gone to bed with the other night. Mousaf Amar, head of security for the royal family of the small North-African country of Timasur, had made the trip to Florida with King Rajeemh and Queen Azhar, and their two adult children. It was Her Royal Majesty's first visit to the states since an unexpected illness last year, and Lindsey had finally met the regal woman after being on details for the king, Prince Raj, and Princess Tahira. Trident provided additional security for the monarchs whenever they were staying in their Clearwater Beach mansion. And there was something about the dark-skinned, brown-eyed Amar—everyone called him by his surname—that made the female operative's heart race, and girlie-parts stand up and take notice.

It'd been a long time since she'd felt an instant attraction to a man, but that's what had happened when she'd first met Amar six months ago, when Princess Tahira had been in town. Lindsey had walked into the Trident conference room where her team, Ian, Amar, and Brody Evans from the Alpha Team were preparing for a briefing about an event the princess was attending. While all heads had turned at her arrival, and her team busted her chops about the female-cut tuxedo she was wearing, a warmth of awareness had come over her. It'd been the result of the appreciative gaze coming from the one person in the room she hadn't met yet. Amar's eyes had roamed her body, setting off tingles and goosebumps, and hell, that was from ten feet away.

When Brody had introduced them, Amar's smooth-as-silk voice had mesmerized her. It'd taken everything in her to remember where they were and why they were there. Since that night, the two of them had danced around each other whenever Amar had been in Florida—sometimes for days, other times for a week or two. Lindsey wasn't always assigned to the royal detail, but some visits involved public events, and it was easier for her to be with the queen or princess in case either woman needed to use the restroom.

Two other female bodyguards had been recently added to Trident's Personal Security Division, and they'd been on-duty with Lindsey and a few of the company's men the other night. The royal family had attended an invitation-only gala at the Tampa Museum of Art. They'd loaned the museum an exhibit of Timasurian art and artifacts to be displayed for six weeks, and the event had been the big debut.

As they'd been doing over the past few months, Lindsey and Amar had found themselves having intellectual and professional conversations before and during the detail. What had been different this time was they'd met for a drink after both their assignments had ended for the night. One thing led to another, and they'd ended up at her apartment around 3:00 a.m.

While I fished my keys out of my purse, Amar clutched my hips and pulled my ass flush against his groin, then nibbled on my neck. The heat of his mouth sent delicious chills down my spine as I tilted my head to the side to give him easier access. His lips were soft, but I could feel the power in them that could take me to amazing heights of ecstasy. It was pure seduction at its finest. With the distraction, it took me longer to locate my keychain, but I was determined to find it and move this party inside where we didn't have to worry about prying eyes.

"Sei una donna molto bella," he whispered in my ear as my hand closed around the keys and I triumphantly pulled them from the bag. I'd learned over the past few months, that in addition to his military training, Amar had attended Harvard for two years before finishing up his degree in Italy. Schooled in both Eastern and Western cultures, he spoke five languages fluently, and each one sounded like foreplay to me no matter what he was saying when he spoke—even if I didn't understand the words.

Opening the door, I hoped like hell I wasn't violating any company rules. The Sawyers had made it perfectly clear that the flirtatious Princess Tahira was off-limits to the men of Trident, but never had anything been said about her head of security. Technically, he wasn't their client, the royal family was, and it wasn't as if I was going to walk into work tomorrow and announce I'd slept with the man. Although if his form of seduction was any indication of how he fucked, I may not be able to keep a silly "I got laid" look off my face.

When the door shut, Amar pinned me against a wall in the small foyer, and his mouth descended on mine. As our tongues tangled, I dropped my purse, and we both began to disarm ourselves. Safeties were engaged on the guns before they thumped to the carpeted floor along with our holsters, extra ammo, and knives. We then reached up to undress each other. As much as I wanted to rip the crisp, dress shirt from his sculpted torso, I figured he couldn't return to the Clearwater Beach mansion that way. My fingers fumbled along the buttons as the room filled with the sounds of our heavy breathing.

Once our suit jackets and shirts were off, Amar reached into one of my bra cups and lifted my breast free. Bending down, he took the taut nipple into his mouth and laved it with attention from his tongue, teeth, and lips. My head fell back against the wall as I dug my nails into his muscular back, eliciting a groan from him. It vibrated through my skin and went straight to my core, increasing my desire.

While one hand held my breast aloft for him, his other trailed down to where I was hot, wet, and wanting. I lifted one knee to his hip and ground my pelvis into his palm. Through my dress pants, his fingers teased me, and I begged for more—almost incoherently. "Please, Amar. Feel . . . you make me . . . feel alive . . . more."

"With pleasure, mia dolce."

His mouth switched to my other breast while he found the button and zipper of my pants. Just as he was about to slide his calloused hand down into my panties, a cell phone rang loudly, and Amar froze, then cursed. "Damn it. I'm sorry, my sweet, but I have to answer that. At 3:00 a.m., it must be important."

I nodded as I gasped for air and relaxed against the wall that was somehow holding me upright, since my knees were quivering with excitement and need. I was pleased to see he seemed just as affected as he caught his breath. "I-It's okay. I understand." Probably more than any other woman he'd ever been with.

Taking a step back, he bent at the waist and grabbed his

jacket from the floor, quickly locating his cell before it stopped ringing. Without looking at the screen, he answered the call in a frustrated bark. "Amar."

After a few moments of him asking questions and then getting answers, I realized our night was over before we ever got to the really good parts. Disconnecting the call, he gazed at me with eyes filled with desire and regret. He reached up and cupped my chin, brushing his thumb over my cheek. "I'm so sorry, mia dolce. A bomb threat was called into the mansion. They're evacuating, and I need to be there."

Turning my head slightly, I pressed my lips against his warm palm. My voice was still husky as I said, "I understand. Do you need help? I can follow you there."

He shook his head. "Thank you, but no. You've had a long night. Climb into bed and dream of me." After kissing me gently on the lips then my forehead, he quickly got dressed and was gone.

"Hey, AAAboooott!"

She startled at Foster calling her name in classic Lou Costello style and glared at him. "What, Shades?" The team had all agreed the nickname fit the man to a 'T.'

"Are you coming with us, or do you want to nap for a little while longer?"

Glancing around she realized everyone had finished eating and was geared up. She was the only one still sitting on the ground. "Yeah, I'm coming. I've had all the beauty rest I need. You, on the other hand, look like you could use a few more hours."

"Personally, I think he could have days of beauty sleep and it wouldn't help," Mancini quipped.

As she'd intended, that got the banter and jabs going

again. Standing, she put the remnants of her meal in a plastic bag and sealed it. She tucked it into her deployment bag which she then swung onto her back and picked up her sniper rifle. Within minutes, they were on their way.

Chapter Five

Never had Foster felt so out of shape. Between high school and college sports, the Secret Service, and now Trident, he'd kept his body in peak physical condition over the years. But with the ups and downs of the mountain landscape, and the lower oxygen levels, he felt like he'd spent the past year scarfing down nothing but Big Macs for a documentary of what not to eat. It didn't help that his gut and ass were on fire from the MRE he'd eaten earlier.

The rest of the team had clearly known what was up the first time he'd needed a pit stop, since their laughter echoed off the surrounding landscape. He was obviously going to need to do some research on MREs. It was evident there was a method to choosing which ones were safe to eat. No one else seemed to be in gastrointestinal distress but him. It was as if an alien being had taken up residence in his abdomen and was trying to dig its way out.

Finishing from his third trip into the woods for some

privacy, he joined the others taking their last fifteen minute break of the day. They should be reaching what would be their campsite in another two hours or so. Glancing around, he saw McCabe was on the satellite phone again, most likely with Ian, getting an update on the missing hiker, since they weren't supposed to be using it for non-emergencies.

Taking a seat on a large boulder next to Morrison, Foster pulled the water pouch out of his deployment bag and took a long pull on the straw-like tubing attached to it. "So, how much longer do I have to deal with the fucking shits?"

The man chuckled. "You should be all right by the time we reach camp. Just be glad you didn't have the cheese omelet. That crap gave me the runs for almost twenty-four hours on my first tour of duty. On top of the fact, it was the most disgusting thing ever. Never ate it again. I'd rather starve."

Foster had gotten very comfortable with the team over the past year, dispelling any doubts he'd had about leaving the Secret Service. It'd been a job he'd loved for years, until some bad shit went down about thirty months ago during a trip to Jamaica protecting the Speaker of the House's family on a vacation. The man's twelve-year-old daughter had been the target of an Al Qaeda kidnapping attempt. While Cain had been able to save her, two other agents had been shot and killed. The ensuing investigation revealed that as the supervising agent, he'd done nothing wrong, but Cain would live the rest of his life knowing two men had died under his command. He'd leapt at the chance to join Trident after he'd heard through US covert spy T. Carter that the company was looking to expand. Foster had gotten to know the man at several top-secret meetings at the White House, and at Club X, an elite, private, BDSM club in the Georgetown area of Washington D.C. Carter was good friends with the original Trident team as well as a Dom at The Covenant. Apparently, he had memberships to lifestyle clubs all over the world. It was amazing how many movers and shakers in politics and business were into kink, and the general public had no idea.

Up until that horrible day when he'd lost two subordinates and almost lost an asset, Cain had been having an ideal life—at least it was his ideal. He'd had a respectable and exciting job and been promoted to supervisor two years prior. His personal life suited him too—the BDSM lifestyle allowed him to get what he needed, when he needed it, and his contracts with submissives always had an end date on them. He'd grown up the child of two very unhappy people who, instead of getting a divorce like normal couples who couldn't stand each other, had stayed together and lived a miserable coexistence. As a result, Cain knew he'd never follow in their footsteps and put a ring on a woman's finger.

He'd discovered the lifestyle ten years ago, at the age of twenty-five. As a new agent, he'd been assigned to help protect a visiting foreign dignitary for a month. The man had a dark, sexual appetite, and his security detail had been required to accompany him to Club X. Guarding the asset there on numerous occasions, Cain had discovered a whole new world he'd never known existed. While he wasn't drawn to the darker play, the milder power exchanges suited him perfectly. After the detail was over, he'd filled out a membership application for the same club. Upon having it approved, he'd apprenticed under a few more experienced Doms until he'd learned and tried every type of play that had called to him.

The lifestyle grounded him. It also gave him the chance to have temporary hookups, with a contract, an end date, and no expectations of him beyond that. Long-term relationships weren't his thing. If that meant he'd eventually die alone, so be it. With any luck, he'd go out in a blaze of glory one week before retirement, whenever that might be.

When McCabe disconnected the call, it drew Cain's attention. "Did they find her yet?"

His teammate shook his head. "No. The dogs lost her scent, but the direction they were heading in was almost straight for us. The weird thing is, they haven't found a single trace of her beyond the scent. No sign of her backpack, camera, or anything else she had with her."

"Maybe she doesn't want to be found," Knight said. "Any chance she's mentally ill or suicidal?"

Again, McCabe shook his head. "Not according to the family. Her uncle's the local sheriff, and Ian said it would be extremely out of character if she disappeared on her own. Anyway, if we do cross paths with her, it will probably be sometime tomorrow. Let's load up and get moving —that is, unless you have to shit again, Shades?"

Foster gave him the middle finger and prayed like hell the man wasn't jinxing him. Hoisting his pack on his back, he adjusted the straps. From the satellite photos and maps they'd studied, they were near the top of a hundred foot cliff they'd have to rappel down in order to make it to the site where they'd be making camp. After free-roping out of the chopper, that sounded like a piece of cake. At the thought, his intestines roared. *Son of a fucking bitch.*

TRUDGING THROUGH THE WOODS, BILLY RAY BROUGHT UP the rear of the motley group. He was sick of living in the wilderness but belonged with his family. Besides, if he went back to civilization, he'd be shot by the cops or thrown in prison thanks to Jessup. It was supposed to have been an easy bank heist, but his asshole brother had killed two people—an off-duty cop, who had the bad luck of being in the wrong place at the wrong time, and a security guard. Now, Billy Ray, Jessup, Darrell, and their father Ross Greenly were wanted by the law and living off the land to avoid a lifetime in prison.

He hadn't wanted to be part of the robbery, but where his father went, he followed. He'd dropped out of high school after failing his freshman year twice. Everyone said he was too stupid to hold down a decent paying job and live on his own, and he agreed with them. He just didn't learn and retain information as easily as most people. Math and stuff got him confused and made his head hurt. So, he had to rely on his father and brothers for money, and robbing people and businesses was how his family made most of their money, but this was the first time they'd hit a bank.

Walking behind Darrell and the girl, he longed to run his fingers through her long, blonde hair. He thought she was so pretty—not in the way his brothers did. They just wanted to have sex with her. Billy Ray did too, but he also wished he could sit and talk to her, take her to a movie, and have her be his girlfriend. At twenty-one, he'd never had a girlfriend before. Oh, he'd had sex before, usually with one of his brother's girlfriends when they'd been drinking, but he wanted a girl he could call his own. Susan—he loved her name—was just the type of girl he wished was his, but the pretty and smart ones usually wanted nothing to do with a dummy like him.

Thumping overhead indicated another helicopter, this one moving much slower than the earlier one. Darrell grabbed Susan by the arm and pulled her close to one of the massive trees that would hide them from view. Billy Ray, Jessup, and their father did the same. They'd been hiking for about two hours—the girl's family had to know by now she was missing, and search and rescue units had to be looking for her.

As the chopper moved to the east, the noise died down. Darrell swung his rifle at Susan who was on her knees, and she threw her hands up in front of her face in a futile gesture to keep from getting shot. "No!"

Billy Ray was about to yell at his brother not to shoot her, but, in a flash, Jessup's hand shot out, knocking the rifle barrel up in the air. "What the fuck are you doing?"

"What we should have done yesterday, asshole. We should have just fucked her and dumped the body."

Ross Greenly stepped between his two arguing sons and shoved them away from each other. "Knock it off, you pieces of shit! No one's fucking or shooting the girl until we're far from here. If they find her body, they won't stop searching for who killed her. No one knows we're out here, and it's going to stay that way. The money's hidden —after the pigs think we're long gone, we'll get it and then head to Mexico. For now, the girl stays alive and with us. We might need her as a hostage."

Staring at Susan, Billy Ray could see she was terrified —she was pale, wide-eyed, and shaking—and he wished he could go over and comfort her.

"Billy Ray!"

His head whipped up at his father's growl, and he realized he'd missed a few moments of the family conversation. "Yeah, Pa?"

"Bring the girl. You two idiots, go lay a few false trails to throw off the fucking cops, then circle back around to the secondary camp."

His brothers didn't seem happy about that, but when Ross Greenly laid down the law, his sons obeyed—it was either that or get their asses kicked.

As Jessup and Darrell headed back the way they'd come, Billy Ray stepped over to Susan and helped her up. His father started in the direction of their next campsite, and they fell in behind him. They'd set up three campsites prior to the bank robbery in case they had to lay low until the heat died down instead of heading straight to Mexico —Jessup's itchy trigger finger had ensured the backup plan had been needed.

Susan tripped over a tree root, and Billy Ray grabbed her upper arm to keep her from falling. Once she was steady again, she glanced at his father's back before returning her gaze to him. A small smile appeared on her pretty face.

"Thanks," she whispered, so Ross didn't hear her. "You're a lot nicer than your brothers are."

Realizing he was still holding her arm, he let go and shrugged. "They're okay. They tease me a lot."

"They shouldn't do that. It's mean."

The corners of his mouth ticked upward. She really was a nice girl. Maybe he could talk his father into letting him keep her. She could go to Mexico with them and be his girlfriend.

"Move it, Billy Ray!"

"Yes, Pa."

Chapter Six

Once his feet hit the ground, Val Mancini disconnected his harness from the rope he'd used to scale down the small cliff. To some, one hundred feet might not be considered small, but rock climbing was one of his favorite recreational pastimes. For him, the sheer face of this cliff had been child's play. As a retired member of the Army Special Forces and FBI's Hostage Rescue Team, he'd climbed and descended many buildings, mountains, and chasms, some more dangerous and exciting than others.

With McCabe unhooking from his own rope next to him, Val tilted his head back to check on Abbott and Foster who'd started their descents. He knew the female sniper could go much faster, but she was keeping an eye on their less experienced teammate. Ian and Devon had made an excellent decision when they'd made McCabe and Foster co-leaders of the team. Val had already been on several assignments with both of them, and each excelled at leadership in their own way. Combined, Val had no trouble taking commands from them.

What he did have trouble with lately was his attraction to country singer Summer Hayes. It wasn't an obsession with a celebrity he'd never met, since she was an occasional visitor to the Trident compound. Instead, it was an obsession with a beautiful woman he couldn't get out of his head. She was a sweet, down-home kind of girl, who made everyone around her feel at ease. She was also a member of The Covenant. While Val and his teammates had all been approved to go into the club, personally, he'd only been inside during the hours it'd been closed. He had no problem with people who enjoyed different kinks in public, it just wasn't for him.

The first time Val had been introduced to Summer a few months ago at a barbecue in the yard between two of the converted warehouses at the Trident compound, he hadn't recognized her as the Grammy winning performer. He'd just seen her as a hot little number who'd piqued his interest. It'd taken almost an hour of talking with her about a variety of subjects before he'd realized she was the singer of several country songs he had on his MP3 player.

Summer was as light and bright as her name suggested, with short, sun-kissed, blonde hair and piercing blue eyes. She was a full foot smaller than his own six three frame and a little skinnier than the women he was normally attracted to, but her personality was what had drawn him in. She'd laughed at his corny jokes and told some good ones right back to him. He'd thought he stood a chance in asking her out, but after she'd had a private conversation with Ian's and Devon's wives later that afternoon, she'd backed off from Val. He started getting the "let's just be friends" body language from her, and the day had ended with her leaving alone and him wondering what the hell had happened.

Shortly after Summer had left, Angie had approached him. It was then he'd learned that the petite singer didn't date out of the lifestyle, and after learning he wasn't in it, she'd thrown up the roadblocks. Who would have thought that *not* being into the BDSM lifestyle would turn a woman off? He'd always thought it would have been the reverse.

The sound of loose rocks coming toward him broke him out of his woolgathering. Jumping back, his gaze went up the cliff in a panic, but relief quickly followed when he saw both Foster and Abbot were still safe and secure with a third of the way left to go. The rocks that had been kicked loose by one of them were small and fell harmlessly at his feet.

Damn it. He knew better than to get distracted during a climb or descent. It was the easiest way to get someone killed. *Well, not on my fucking watch.*

"You okay?" McCabe asked, without taking his eyes off the climbers.

"Yeah. My bad. Zoned out for a sec."

The tight-faced man nodded but remained silent. It was still an official reprimand, non-verbal as it was. *Stay in the game or get the fuck out.*

Once Abbott and Foster were down, Morrison and Knight made quick work of their own descents. It didn't take long for everyone to gear back up, and it was Val's turn to take point. The sounds of their boots crunching on the snow filled the air. Rounding a dense crop of trees and brush, he slammed on the brakes and threw his fist up to shoulder height, stopping everyone behind him and demanding their silence. His heart pounded in his chest, and it took everything in him not to turn tail and run. Keeping his eyes on the big, black, furry mass in from of him, he twisted his head just enough so Foster, who was right behind him, could hear him say in a low and cautious voice, "It's a bear—big motherfucker too."

From the massive size of it, he guessed it was a male, which had its pros and cons. If it wasn't a female, they didn't have to worry about a mother's instinct for protecting her young. However, male black bears could grow to be seven feet tall, standing erect, and usually weighed anywhere from 200 to 300 pounds, but there were some on record which had weighed between 500-600 pounds. While this one wasn't that big, Val estimated it still tipped the scales at close to 400. It would also be very hungry, having just emerged from winter hibernation. Furthermore, black bears could run up to thirty-five miles per hour compared to the average human clocking in at eight miles per hour—so running away from one was rarely a successful option.

The beast's snout was in the hole of a decaying, downed tree, as his huge, right, front paw pulled at the outer bark, trying to make the access larger. The trunk was probably filled with termites, which were on a bear's diet up here in the middle of fucking nowhere.

Val signaled for everyone to back up slowly—they would need to find a way around the animal. Trying not to make any sudden moves, he reached back and pulled the canister of bear spray from an outer pocket of his deployment bag. Brody Evans had ordered enough for everyone to carry, just in case. Shooting and killing a bear was to be avoided at almost every cost. While the American black bear wasn't on the federal endangered list, no one wanted to harm the animal unnecessarily.

Taking a step backward, he kept his eyes on the beast. A few more feet and he should be good. Val was just about to sigh in relief when his heel came down hard on a twig and the snap seemed to echo around him. The bear's head came up with a grunt, and his gaze found the intruder right away.

Fuck.

The bear sniffed and grunted again, then lifted up onto his hind legs and let out a roar that would make some people piss their pants. If Val wasn't armed to the teeth, with his team on his heels as backup, he may have been one of those people. This was definitely a huge example of the species.

The first rule of bear encounters was don't panic—check. The second was don't run—double check. The third rule was talk to the beast in a calm voice and make yourself look as big as possible. Yelling could trigger an attack. If all went well by this point, and you were still alive, then move slowly and sideways, away from the bear. You could see where you were going and still not seem threatening.

Val took a deep breath and stood tall, lifting his arms out to the side. "Hey, Smokey, good bear. We're not here to hurt you or take your dinner away. Finish eating, and we'll take the long way around. All right?"

The bear bellowed and stood his ground. From somewhere behind Val, McCabe softly said, "Costello's got that big head in her sights. If he rushes you, dive to your right, and she'll take the shot if she has to."

That was the last thing any of them wanted, but it was nice to know that either way, he wasn't going to wrestle with the damn thing. Val thought about throwing it a shit-producing MRE to eat as a distraction, but that'd probably be considered animal abuse. Moving slowly to his right, he kept talking. "Good, Smokey. Or do you prefer Pooh Bear or Yogi?"

The enormous beast dropped down on his front legs again and pawed at the ground. Val braced himself for a charge, but thankfully, it didn't come. Swinging its head side to side, the bear watched as the human intruder got further and further away, then finally went back to his dinner. Once the team was a good distance away, they regrouped, and Val took some much needed oxygen into his lungs.

Knight slapped him on his back and laughed. "If Romeo didn't fit you so well, we'd be calling you Boo-Boo from now on." His voice dropped. "Hey, Boo-Boo. Let's go steal a pic-a-nic basket. Hey-ey-ey-ey."

Grinning, Val gave his buddy the finger. "Fuck you, man. I'll be the first one to admit my fucking knees are shaking, and I'm sure yours would be too if you'd been on point."

"Let's find out," McCabe said with a chuckle. "Batman, you're on point, while pretty boy recovers from his run-in with the big teddy bear."

The retired SEAL rolled his eyes. "Fuck."

THE FOREST STIRRED AROUND MALLORY. IT WAS DAWN, AND the nocturnal creatures were getting ready to sleep, while the rest of the animals and birds were starting their day. Birds chirped and squirrels scurried, searching for their breakfast. Jessup's snores reached her ears. Darrell and Ross—Billy Ray had told her his father's name yesterday—had left the camp before sunrise to lay some more false trails for her potential rescuers. Billy Ray was sleeping about five feet from her, and Jessup was on the other side of the fire that had died out hours ago. They were supposed to be guarding her, but both had succumbed to slumber again after the others had left, believing Mallory was secured with the zip tie and rope around her waist. What they hadn't realized was she'd been working the knot loose for the past few hours and was finally untied. Her wrists were still restrained but she could easily break the zip tie later. First, she needed to get the hell out of there.

Slowly rolling to her side, she tried to make as little noise as possible so as to not wake the men. Pushing up onto her knees, she paused a moment and observed them. Neither one moved or opened their eyes. She wanted to go north, but that would mean walking past them, and the others had gone in that direction earlier, so instead, she'd go east and then loop around when she could. Awkwardly getting to her feet, she tiptoed away, avoiding any twigs that might snap and alert her captors.

She'd gotten about fifty feet into the woods when she heard Billy Ray shout, "Hey!"

Damn it.

Taking off at a full run, she didn't even glance back as Jessup cursed. "Fuck! Get her!"

Mallory dodged past trees and shrubs, hurdling some downed limbs, ignoring the stiffness in her legs. She needed to get as far away as possible before finding a place to hide for a few moments to rid herself of the zip tie. Her heart pounded in her chest as the men made no attempt to hide the sounds of them chasing her. Her foot hit something, and she stumbled but regained her balance and kept running. Cutting to her right, she did as her dad had taught her, zig-zagging instead of running straight. As she passed a thicket of shrubs, several birds flew from it, startling her, but she just ducked her head and kept going. Her dad's voice resounded in her mind. *Run, Mal. Keep running. Don't look back. Dodge to the right, then to the left again—no set pattern. Take a route that'll be difficult for them. You can see what's ahead, but they won't be focusing on the terrain, they'll be looking at you. Find a weapon as soon as you can and don't be afraid to use it. Swing a branch or rock to kill. Don't worry about the consequences. It's self-defense. If they get close, use your hands, fingers, feet, knees, elbows, and head to attack. Go on the offensive—they won't expect it.*

There were so many other things he'd taught her and her brothers, practicing different self-defense and E&E— evade and escape—techniques whenever they had a chance. If she had a moment to analyze it all, she'd be shocked at how natural it had become. She didn't puzzle over what she needed to do, she just did it.

"Go that way, you fucking idiot! Get her!" Jessup sounded beyond pissed, and she didn't want to focus on what he'd probably do if he caught her.

Mallory's feet struck the earth as she scanned the harsh landscape in front of her. The terrain was sloping upward. She needed to find a way to head in the other direction. A twig snapped behind her. Someone was getting closer, but she didn't dare take a peek to see who it was and how much distance was between them.

Pivoting to the left, she was about to jump over another large tree limb when she was tackled from behind. Arms wrapped around her waist, and Mallory twisted to her right, using the person's momentum to keep him moving past her. They went down, but thanks to her adjustment, she landed on top of his chest, knocking the air from his lungs. His grip loosened, and she scrambled to her feet.

Even though her wrists were restrained, she could still use her hands. Picking up a hefty branch, she spun around to see Jessup trying to stand. With all her might, she aimed for his head, but he saw it coming and ducked. Her weapon collided with his shoulder and the back of his neck, dropping him hard to the ground again. A moan escaped him even though his body went still. She hefted the branch to hit him again, but the sound of someone approaching fast, had her spinning around.

Billy Ray ran toward her and stopped a few feet away, eyeing the defensive stance she took. She didn't want to hurt him—he wasn't like the others—but she would if she had to. His gaze went from her to his unconscious brother and back again.

Holding the tree branch in front of her, she pleaded with him. "Please, Billy Ray. Let me go. They're going to rape and kill me. Please, I have a family I love and want to see again. Please."

Her vision blurred with unshed tears, and she blinked them away. Billy Ray hesitated and glanced at Jessup again before seemingly making his decision. He pointed to his left. "Go that way. I'll tell him you went in the other direction. Look for the river and follow it—it'll get you back home. Hurry."

Despite hoping he would help her, she was surprised when he did. "Th-thank you."

He nodded, the expression on his face softening. "I wish you could have been my girlfriend." Jessup's moan had them starting, but he was still down for the count. Billy Ray waved his hand to the east. "Hurry. Before he wakes up."

Mallory didn't need to be told again. She took off at a full run.

Chapter Seven

Darius stretched in his sleeping bag, then listened to the sounds around him. His internal clock told him it was around 0630 hours. He heard murmuring coming from the clearing next to the rock shelter they'd slept under. Tents had been out of the question for this training mission, since it was highly unlikely they'd have them during a real one. Glancing around, he saw Romeo and Skipper still supine with their eyes shut, but the spaces Abbott, Foster, and McCabe had slept in were now empty. While he'd love to close his eyes for another ten or fifteen minutes, his bladder couldn't wait.

This weekend was a lot more pleasurable than the last one. He'd been stuck on the "princess" detail which sucked royal donkey shit. Princess Tahira had attended a big gala at the Tampa Museum of Art with her parents, brother, and a few members of their extended family. Darius had drawn one of the short straws and been assigned to Tahira. She was a huge flirt with her single bodyguards and could be a first class brat when she wanted to be—which was more often than not. The gorgeous twenty-four-year-old was off-limits to anyone employed or contracted by Trident—and she knew it too. But that didn't stop her from propositioning anyone not wearing a wedding ring or who she knew was engaged. However, Boss-man seemed to have a soft spot for the princess, always greeting her warmly, and Darius had no idea why. All he knew was it was a pain in the ass to guard her and brush off her advances at the same time. More than once he'd ended up with a twitching cock around her. He'd have to be dead or gay not to have a reaction to the exotic beauty.

Crawling out of his sleeping bag, he checked his boots for spiders before pulling them on. They'd all slept in their camos last night as if it were a real mission. The only spare clothing any of them had was socks and they'd probably all be ripe for a shower when they got back to civilization some time tomorrow morning. It was colder than a witch's tit, but in an hour or so, as the sun rose higher in the sky, it would be much more comfortable. He shook out his jacket and pulled it on.

After a quick trip into the woods to pee like a race-horse, he returned to where Abbott and the others were eating their choice of MREs for breakfast. McCabe's bag was sitting on a rock, and Darius shuffled through the meal packages the man had been carrying until he found one tagged Maple Sausage. The meat, if that's what you wanted to call it, wasn't the greatest, but the maple muffin top and trail mix that came with it were pretty good, in addition to some cheese and crackers he'd save for later.

He sat on a rock next to McCabe. "How far to the next rock face?"

"About three klicks." Translated, that was just under two miles. After that they had about sixteen more miles of high and low terrain but no more sheer cliffs. That didn't mean the rest of their hike was going to be easy, it just meant no more vertical drops.

"Any word on the missing hiker?"

"Still missing as of fifteen minutes ago when I spoke to Boss-man."

Shit. The longer she was out alone in the elements, the less chance they had of finding her alive.

Darius ate his breakfast as Morrison and Mancini joined the group. Within the hour they were all fed, packed up, and on their way again. He'd grown comfortable with his new team over the months since leaving his old one behind. Having served with the TS Alpha Team when they'd all been on SEAL Team Four together, he'd jumped at the chance when word spread that Ian and Devon were adding to their company. At thirty-eight, he'd gotten his twenty years of service in and then gotten the hell out. He was still in excellent condition, and if he stayed that way, he could be with Trident for a good ten years more before retiring. Between his military pension and the dramatic increase in pay in the private sector, he could become a bum on some beach in Florida, or even the Caribbean somewhere, and just fish for the rest of his life. Maybe by then he'll have found someone to settle down with. At least with Trident, once a mission was over, they'd return home immediately instead of sitting in the sandbox on the other side of the world waiting to cycle back out to the states. Eight to ten month deployments overseas were now a thing of his past.

On point again, he noticed the tree line opening up

and a rocky expanse just ahead. They were nearing the cliff. As if this were a true mission, the others held back as he moved closer to the edge. It was his job at the moment to make sure it was safe before giving his team the all clear signal. Keeping an eye out for any more bears or possibly a mountain lion, Darius eased toward the rim. He was also studying the terrain in front of him. The last thing he wanted to do was trip and pitch forward over the edge.

When he reached a large boulder, seemingly defying the laws of gravity, at the edge of the ridge, his breath caught at the beauty of the land before him. Majestic mountains surrounded him, under cloudless skies of blue. From there, he could see miles of evergreens, scattered lakes and streams, and snow covered peaks. They'd reached a lower elevation late yesterday afternoon and there were only patches of snow at this level.

He was just about to signal the rest of the team, when a flash of red caught his eye far below him, maybe a half mile from the bluff. His gaze returned to the spot, and he tried to zero in on what was moving. The figure entered a small clearing before disappearing again, but it had been enough for him to register long, blonde hair. The missing hiker.

While most people would have called out to get her attention, years of training had honed his instincts and powers of observation. The girl wasn't just hiking through the woods, she was running . . . and hiding. Something or someone was after her.

Going down on one knee, Darius held up a solid fist at shoulder height, then extended his pointer finger in the air. His team would know to stay low and for one person to ease up stealthily toward him for backup. By the time he'd swung his deployment bag off his back, located his binoculars in the outside pocket, and was lying flat, McCabe was by his side.

"What's up?"

Bringing the binoculars to his eyes, Darius scanned the area below. The glass lenses were specially coated, so he didn't have to worry about sun glare reflecting off them and alerting anyone to the team's presence. "Looks like we found our hiker. Twelve o'clock, about a quarter klick from the base. Problem is she's running scared." A short distance past the girl and to the south, he spotted more movement. Unlike her, this person hadn't been as easy to spot—camouflage would do that. "I've got one male at one o'clock, about half a klick out." He continued his surveillance and, after a full minute had passed, spotted another person even further south but closer to the cliff. "Second tango, probably male as well, two o'clock, a quarter klick out."

"Whoever they are, they're flanking her and driving her in the direction they want her to go. Keep watch." McCabe signaled the rest of the team to put their comm units on, so they could communicate when separated, then move forward and take cover behind the huge boulder.

Darius didn't see anyone else, but something told him there were more out there. He shifted the binoculars back to where he last saw the girl. With that red jacket, she wasn't hard to find—and that was both good and bad.

A male voice rang out from below, echoing off the rock face. "Hey, pretty girl. Come out, come out, wherever you are."

Any chance the men could be rescuers fled his mind. That voice had dripped with pure evil with a hint that its owner found the chase amusing and entertaining. The bastard was letting the poor girl know they weren't far behind her.

Beside him, McCabe gave the team an update, then took the lead and said, "We can't drop from here—we'll be sitting ducks before we're halfway down if they have rifles, which we have to assume they do. I doubt anybody up in these parts is without one. Abbott and Mancini, scopes out, keep an eye on these guys. Shades, take watch over the girl—I need Batman to fly with me." Foster crawled over to Darius who handed over his binoculars. He pointed out where he'd been watching the red coat and made sure the other man had the girl in his sights before turning to McCabe.

Their leader pointed to the left. "Cowboy, check the north end of the ridge—see if we can rappel down without being spotted. Batman check the south. Find a way down and fast."

Using boulders, grottos, bushes, and trees as cover, Darius worked his way along the edge of the cliff but after a few hundred feet, he realized there was no way down that didn't put them in plain sight or wasn't a potential death trap. Thankfully, Reese's voice came over the comm in his ear stating he'd found a spot.

Darius returned to his team to find McCabe already pulling out what they'd need. "Cowboy, Batman, Skipper, you're with me. Romeo and Costello, keep your eyes on the tangos until we find out what the hell is going on, and watch for others. Shades, don't let that girl out of your sights. Move out."

Reese led the way back to where the bluff curved around and inward. As long as they hadn't missed anyone on the east side of the girl, then they shouldn't have any problem getting down fast without being spotted. While Darius and Kip got their harnesses on and rubbed dirt over their faces for additional camouflage, the other two men anchored two ropes to a nearby tree using single-loop figure eights and locking carabiners. This descent was going to be much faster than yesterday's in that it was used by special ops teams and search and rescue units to reach a victim or target quickly. As McCabe dropped the ropes off the cliff and made sure they weren't tangled or caught on anything, Reese double-checked Darius and Kip's harnesses and the anchors. Within minutes, the two rappelers were on their way down with their rifles strung across their backs and nothing else unless it fit in the pockets of their camo jackets or tactical pants.

Foster's voice came over the comm units when they were halfway down. "She's moving east, about the same distance out. Heading toward your twelve o'clock." That meant she was almost directly behind them.

With his knees bent, the rope taut in his hands, Darius bounced off the face of the bluff with his feet, dropped about five yards, then repeated the process. Kip was about eight feet to his right, doing the same thing.

When their boots hit the ground, they quickly unhooked from the rope, and Darius spoke into his microphone. "We're down. Where's our girl?"

"Just passing your twelve o'clock, about two hundred fifty yards out."

Despite the seriousness of the situation, there were a few chuckles, followed by Mancini saying, "In klicks, ya damn civilian." Never having served in the military, Foster still couldn't get used to the mile-to-klick conversions, and they were always busting his ass for it.

"Knock it off," McCabe ordered without any heat. Jokes were par for the course on missions to help ease any tension. "Skipper and Batman, see if you can intercept without alerting the tangos to our presence. Cowboy's on his way down."

"Copy, Duracell." Darius scrambled over a rock expanse in silence with Kip on his heels. They soon faded into the tree line, their camo clothing matching their surroundings. The lookouts above would let them know if there were any changes in either Mallory's location or the two men after her.

"Shift to your eleven o'clock, Batman."

He made the adjustment Foster had given him, keeping an eye out for the tell-tale red coat and any sign of danger. The hair on the back of his neck tingled, and once again, his instincts were telling him there were more tangos out here then they'd spotted so far. He just hoped he and Kip reached Mallory before someone else did.

HIDING BEHIND A TREE, MALLORY TRIED TO CATCH HER breath as she scanned the area she'd just come from. It was almost as if they were playing a game of cat and mouse with her. She kept trying to turn north, but each time she did, she'd either hear or spot one of the men—they weren't exactly being quiet about stalking her—and have to turn back in the other direction. A few times she'd heard Jessup call out to her, "Hey, pretty girl. Come out, come out wherever you are."

The fucking creep.

She'd obviously not hit him hard enough, damn it. Darrell was also out there somewhere—she'd caught a glimpse of him earlier. Either Billy Ray had lied about sending them in the other direction or they hadn't believed him—not that it mattered at this point.

After Billy Ray had let her go, she'd run for a good twenty minutes before taking a moment to break out of the zip ties. The trick her dad taught her had worked. The key to snapping them was to make them as tight as possible, using your teeth to pull the one end sticking out, and then make sure the locking mechanism is on top and between your wrists. Then you lifted your arms above your head and brought them down fast toward your abdomen, simulating an attempt in getting your shoulder blades to touch each other. Your elbows needed to flare out like chicken wings. If you did all that properly, the restraint should snap at its weakest point—the locking mechanism. Thankfully, that's exactly what'd happened.

Now with a huge cliff to the west and the men to the north and east, her only option was to head south. The problem was, she'd gotten so far away from any areas she'd explored over the years with her dad, she had no idea what she was heading towards. All she knew was she had to keep going, otherwise she'd be raped then most likely killed when they finally tired of her, and she'd be damned if she'd go down without a fight. But if she didn't find some fresh water soon, dehydration would begin to take its toll, in addition to the heavy snowfall and colder temperatures she'd figured were coming her way. The sun had been swallowed by dark clouds about a half hour ago, and the scent of foul weather had settled around her. It wouldn't be long before snowflakes drifted down from the sky.

She'd been running for about two hours, and the only reason she hadn't passed out from the exertion yet was the fact she'd been a cross country runner since her freshman year in high school. While she no longer competed, she'd kept up her routine of five miles twice a week and two miles three times a week.

Something rustled behind her, and she gasped and spun to see two squirrels chasing each other. *Thank God.*

Turning back, she took stock of where the sun was, then wondered if she should try and head northeast again. If she could just get past them and continue in that direction, she'd eventually come to a river she could then follow east toward Ouray. By this point, she was probably closer to the little town than where she'd parked her car, and trying to go back the way she came would most likely end up getting her spotted by one of the men.

One more check of the directions she thought the men were in, and then she'd make another run for it, now that her breathing was under control. As she peeked around the tree, a female deer was the only large thing she saw moving. But just as Mallory prepared to take off again, a gloved hand closed around her mouth and another around her waist.

Oh, no! They found me!

Struggling to get loose, she reached back to scratch her assailant's face, but his head was moving too much for her to do any damage. Whoever it was, she'd never heard him approach. Her feet left the ground, and she kicked back, but the man crushed her against the tree to keep her immobile.

Hot air brushed against her ear a split second before a low voice ordered, "Mallory, calm down. I'm here to help." The words didn't immediately register, and she continued to thrash. "Damn it, Mallory. Your uncle sent us to find you. Stop struggling or the guys who are after you will hear."

That time she understood, and her frantic movements ceased. She sagged with relief. He knew her real name—it wasn't one of those bastards. Someone had found her. She was safe. God, she hoped she was safe.

"I'm going to let go, okay?" he whispered. "Turn around but stay quiet."

Mallory nodded, and his hands released her. She wasn't sure what she expected when she faced him, but it wasn't what she saw. The man was about six foot two with broad shoulders and russet colored hair peeking out of the black knit cap he wore, as well as across his jaw and upper lip. He was covered in camouflage clothing and had spread dirt over his face. Even with the sweat and grime, she could tell he was incredibly handsome. She also didn't miss the assault rifle on his back sticking out over his right shoulder, nor the gentleness in his soft, brown eyes, which were assessing her.

"Are you hurt?"

She shook her head—it was obvious a few bumps, bruises, and blisters weren't what he was asking about.

"Good. How many men are out there, and why are they chasing you?"

Keeping her voice as low as his, she answered, "Four. They robbed a bank the other day and killed a guard and a cop. It was all over the news. I ran into two of them while hiking and . . . and they kidnapped me. It's a father and his three sons. The father was pissed they took me but wouldn't let me go. They were planning on taking me somewhere . . ." She swallowed hard. ". . . to rape and then k-kill me, but he wanted them out of the area where rescuers would be looking for me first. We have to get out of here. They've been chasing me and letting me know it. If they see you, they'll kill you, I'm sure."

She turned to lead him toward the river, but his hand on her arm stopped her short. Her eyes narrowed at him. "What? We have to run."

"Not until my team takes care of the bad guys."

"Team? What team?" *There are more rescuers out here? Thank God.* Unless they got hurt saving her.

Movement to her left caught her attention, and another man, similarly camouflaged, appeared next to the first. With light brown hair, he was about two inches shorter than the redhead, and a little thinner, but definitely in excellent shape. His hazel eyes were sharp on the woods behind her. Unlike his partner, his rifle was in his hands. Neither man answered her question, and Red put a hand to his ear. It took a moment for her to realize he had an earpiece and was listening to whatever was being said over it.

He retrieved his weapon from his back, then grabbing her upper arm, he pulled her past him and propelled her forward. "Gotta move. Unfriendlies are headed this way."

The other man stayed behind as Mallory was led away, and she was worried about him. It would be four against one. She tried to glance back over her shoulder to see where he was, but Red's massive body blocked her view. "But we can't leave him alone."

"No buts, sweetheart. And don't worry, Skipper's not alone. We train for this stuff. It's the bad guys who should be worried. Now let's get you hidden."

After a few dozen yards, he tucked her behind a boulder surrounded by thick bushes. Taking a tactical position next to her, he eyed the area they'd just come from, then glanced at her and frowned. He reached over and flipped the hem of her coat over. "Take it off and turn it inside out. That red is like a neon sign. At least the underside is mostly black."

Damn, why hadn't she thought about that? *Stupid. Stupid. Stupid.* She quickly unbuttoned it and took it off, pulling the sleeves through themselves. He was right. Even though the collar, placket, and hem were red, the rest was all black. She donned the inside-out coat and looked at him.

Once again, he reached over and, this time, tucked the collar down into the coat, then nodded. "Better."

"Thanks. So, do you have a name, or should I just call you Rambo?" She probably shouldn't even be whispering, but since he was, it must be okay. She always jabbered when she was nervous.

The corners of his mouth ticked up as he kept watch of their surroundings. "Darius Knight, but my teammates call me Batman."

An unexpected grin spread across her face. The fact that he was military and not just someone from search and rescue unit finally sank in. His weapon wasn't a hunting rifle, but instead, was a military-grade assault rifle. Maybe the bad guys *were* the ones who should be worried about what they were heading into. "Cool nickname. My dad's a retired Marine. What branch are you?"

"Navy. SEAL to be exact, but I'm out now and in the private sector. My team and I were dropped in by helicopter for a training mission. We received word yesterday to keep an eye out for you."

He paused, his hand going to his ear. His smile dropped, and he brought his finger to his lips before motioning for her to get low behind the rock and shrubs. Mallory's heart pounded in her chest while a shiver coursed through her body. And, damn it, now was not the time to really need to pee.

CHAPTER EIGHT

With McCabe on his six, Logan Reese melted into the woods. As had been the norm for the past few months working cases and missions with Trident, he couldn't help the anxiousness from building within him. He still had no idea why Ian and Devon Sawyer had taken a risk by hiring him. And, yes, it was a huge risk. Having been a prisoner of war in Afghanistan for a week, over two years ago, and listening to his team being brutalized and then slaughtered still weighed heavily on his mind and soul. Only one other of his fellow Marines, out of seven captives, had been alive when another team of Marines, joined by some Navy SEALs, had swooped in to rescue them. Logan had been just hours away from being the next man cruelly murdered.

Again, he had no idea why the Sawyer brothers had taken a chance on him, but he knew if he fucked up just once, he'd be gone—if he didn't end up dead first. If that happened, he prayed none of his teammates lost their lives too.

Upon hiring him, Ian had added several non-negotiable stipulations to his job contract. One was that he saw a psychologist trained in treating people with PTSD three times a week when he wasn't away on an assignment. The second mandatory requirement was sitting down with his team and recounting his horror story. If he was going to be their backup, they had every right to know all about the man covering their six. While he'd understood the reasoning behind it, doing it had been very difficult. His mind flashed back to that meeting.

I eyed my new team as they sat around the conference table waiting to find out what this meeting was all about. The door was closed and the only other people in the room besides Omega Team were Lindsey, who was splitting her time being the sniper for both teams, and Ian and Devon. The two bosses knew everything I was about to say, and it made things a little easier to have them there for support.

Ian leaned forward on his elbows at the far end of the table. "We waited to have this meeting until you had a few months training together and getting to know each other. As you know, we hand-picked all of you based on your experience, leadership abilities, integrity, and ability to get the damn job done no matter what. You've all proven yourselves to be the best of the best among your peers, and that's why you're here. But everyone in our world has had bad experiences in one form or another. Unless you're a wet-behind-the-ears FNG, you've seen and lived through some really bad shit at one point or another. Agreed?" FNG was military lingo for the fucking new guy, and if you had that tag, you had to wait for your team to come up with a nickname for you.

Everyone in the room nodded. I'd heard the stories of some of the shit my teammates had gone through during either their time in the military or their jobs in law enforcement or both. But as far as I knew, not one of them had been held prisoner by the enemy for seven fucking days and listened as their teammates were murdered while wondering which one of them was next.

Screams from long ago resonated in my head, and I forced them into a mental box and slammed the lid shut. I'd deal with them later—right now, I had to come clean to my team and pray they still wanted to work with me, because it was highly unlikely anyone else would want to hire me with my baggage.

It took a moment for me to realize that silence hung in the room and everyone was staring at me. My gaze found Ian's, and the boss nodded at me. It was time.

Clearing my dry throat, I leaned forward. "Um . . ." I took a deep breath and let it out slowly. "What I'm about to say is probably going to shock the shit out of you—"

Mancini snorted. "If you're going to tell us you're really a woman, it doesn't matter. Costello's already broken us in."

Chuckles filled the air, and a little tension left my body . . . but not enough. "Yeah, that's not it. I . . . uh . . . I was a POW for a week in the sandbox. While I can't tell you about what my team and I were doing before we were ambushed, or where exactly we were, I'll tell you what I can."

Any levity in the room vanished. I kept my gaze on Ian. For some reason, talking to my normally sarcastic and sometimes acerbic boss was making it easier to recount my horror story for everyone else. "It was a little over two years ago. Like I said, we walked into an ambush. Not sure if it was bad intel or bad timing—either way, it didn't matter. We were outnumbered— about a hundred against twelve. We lost five men in the initial attack. With no way out, we surrendered, hoping an opportunity to escape would present itself or a rescue would come.

Neither happened. At least not for seven days. We were moved around over the first twenty-four hours before we ended up in a camp. We were shackled and thrown into cells."

A chill went down my spine. I was no longer in the conference room. Instead, I was back in the rustic building, searching for a way to get out, and wondering if I'd ever see my family again. "We were there maybe an hour or two. Couldn't be sure since they took everything except our pants. Moonshine was the first one to be dragged back outside." I couldn't even tell my new team the real names of my murdered teammates. They were classified, so all I could use to refer to them was their nicknames. "He got a few good punches in when they were taking him from his cell, but one of the bastards cracked his skull with a piece of wood. I'd like to say that was the worst of it, but it wasn't. We had to listen to him get whipped for what seemed like fucking hours. I'll never forget how he tried not to scream, but soon it was probably involuntary."

A few muttered curses came from the Omega team. At some point Lindsey, who was sitting to my right, placed a reassuring hand on my arm. She gave it a light squeeze as I found the courage to continue. "Again, I wish that was the worst part. When the sound of the whip and the screams stopped, the rest of us just looked at each other, trying to figure out what the fuck was happening. The door swung open, and we expected them to bring Moonshine back in." I swallowed hard and couldn't contain the quiver that developed in my voice. "All they brought back in was his head."

Gasps and curses, which were no longer muttered, filled the room. Ian stood, grabbed a bottle of water from a small fridge, and handed it to me. Opening it, I guzzled three-quarters of it, before wiping away the tears I hadn't realized were rolling down my cheeks.

"I still have flashbacks to being in that fucking cell, hearing the crack of a whip over and over again, mixed in with my teammates yelling in pain, as one by one they were fucking tortured. I can still hear those fucking pricks taunting us, even though I didn't understand most of what they were saying. But the worst was when the cries of agony faded and then disappeared altogether. Then the fucking celebration would start. Shouts to Allah and guns being fired in the air were followed by those fucking bastards carrying one of my buddies' detached head by the hair into the cell area for the rest of us to see what they'd done to him. Chained like fucking dogs, we had no chance to escape. The second day we were there, one of my guys managed to get loose, but before he could free the rest of us, two guards walked in and sprayed his legs with bullets from an assault rifle. He was still alive but unable to walk, and they fucking dragged him outside. Two hours later . . ." From the expressions on my current team's faces as they sat around the conference table, they already knew why I couldn't finish that sentence. I was too choked up to repeat what had happened to my friend Danny Coleman, and the last memory I had of him was just his head.*

"How many of you made it back?" Morrison asked quietly.

"Only one of my buddies and I were still alive when a joint rescue team managed to come in and get us. There wasn't a fucking tango left alive in the camp by the time it was over, and we managed to recover the bodies of my teammates and bring them home." I wiped the salty tears from my eyes again. *"Look, I know this is far from what you expected to hear, and I know you've got to be wondering what the hell I'm doing on this team and will I be able to cover your six. I do have flashbacks, but since I've been on US soil, they've only come when I'm sleeping. I've been seeing a shrink several times a week since I've been*

back and it's going well. I honestly was shocked when Ian and Dev offered me the job, but I'll tell you this . . . I'll be damned if I ever have to bury another teammate—especially if it's because I'm the weakest link. I've got your six no matter what. But if you're not comfortable with that, tell me now, and I'll resign." It was the last thing I wanted to do. Working for Trident had given me a purpose in life again—a reason to get up every morning. If I was sitting in a recliner watching TV for the rest of my life, that would probably send me to a rubber room long before my PTSD did.

I stood. "Unless you have any more questions, I'll wait outside while you talk this over with each other. Whatever you all decide is best for the team, I'll understand."

Shutting the door behind me, I made a beeline to the men's room at the end of the hall. Splashing water onto my face, I washed away the evidence of my tears. I stared at my reflection. Long gone was the eighteen-year-old kid I'd been when I'd enlisted in the Marines. Missing was the cocky twenty-two-year-old man going through the Individual Training Course (ITC)—the intense, seven-month course to become one of the elite Marine Corps Forces Special Operations Command Critical Skills Operators (MARSOC CSO). Vanished was the man who'd never experienced the worst that another human could inflict on his fellow man in the name of Allah, God, or whoever they worshiped.

Gathering my composure again, I strode back out and stood in the hall, waiting for the team's decision. It was about ten minutes before the door opened and Devon gestured for me to come back in. As I took my seat again, I tried to read the expressions on my teammates' faces, but no one was giving me any indication on how the vote had gone.

McCabe crossed his arms over his massive chest. "I have to admit, I was a little pissed at the bosses here for not dropping this bomb on the team earlier. That being said, I do understand their rationalization. Each one of us has been on a few cases and missions with you over the past, what? eight or nine months, and none of us have seen anything that had us worried about you watching our six. You've proven yourself, that's for sure. The vote was unanimous for you to stay on the team on one condition."

Relief shot through me. I'd do anything to stay on the team. "What's that?"

"If you ever feel like you can't do a mission or if you feel like your PTSD is going to rear its fucking ugly head during one, you've got to let one of us know, man. We can't read minds. But if you tell us, we can work around it. Don't make any of us regret our decision. Understood?"

I nodded and glanced at each of my teammates, making sure I didn't see any reluctance or, God forbid, pity in their expressions. But neither emotion showed. All I saw was understanding and acceptance. "Understood. I won't let you down."

Grinning, Lindsey said, "And we won't let you down, Cowboy."

A twig cracking had him silently swiveling his head to the right—no one on his team would have made a mistake like that. Using a large pine as cover, he hung his rifle across his back, and pulled his Sig Sauer out of his holster. Thank God they were armed as if this had been a real mission. In close quarters, the rifle could be snatched out of his hand easier than a pistol.

As a lone, camouflaged figure crept into view, Logan shifted, so he wouldn't be spotted until it was too late. This was one of the many maneuvers that had been ingrained in him over years of training and active missions. It was muscle memory, and he did it without conscious thought.

Two more steps and Logan would be in position to surprise the man with a 9mm to the temple. But the bastard suddenly stopped. He was listening for trouble, maybe even sensed the danger he was walking into.

The thump of a stone landing to the man's left had him spinning around, and that was all Logan needed to take him off-guard. "Unless you want your brains to be squirrel food, drop the weapon and link your fingers behind your head."

The guy had frozen in place as soon as the first few threatening words had been spoken and the barrel of the Sig had touched the back of his head. But by the time Logan had finished giving the orders, he'd followed them to a T.

Over the man's shoulder, Logan saw McCabe morph from the surrounding foliage with a grin on his face and his own pistol in his hand. In a low voice, the team leader commented, "Always amazes me how idiots fall for a rock thrown past them. You got zips on you?"

"Yeah." Holstering his weapon again, he retrieved a plastic zip tie from one of his cargo pants pockets. With practiced precision, he restrained the man's wrists at his lower back, then removed several weapons from various places on his body. "Where're your buddies?"

"Fuck you, asshole. You'll be dead as soon as they find you."

"Yeah, I highly doubt that, fucktard."

McCabe spoke into his comms. "One tango secured. Where's the second one?"

"Lost him in some trees about two klicks from my twelve o'clock," their female sniper responded.

"Keep watch. Shades and Romeo, send down the packs, then come join the party."

The two men acknowledged the order, then Knight's voice came over the airwaves and gave them the intel he'd gotten moments before. "Costello, according to our asset, there are three more tangos including the one you had eyes on. Rifles, side arms, and knives, so watch your sixes."

"Copy that," Lindsey responded. "Scanning for them, but there's a lot of cover for them down there."

Hitching a thumb to the east, McCabe said, "Lock him down with Batman and guard the girl. I'll meet up with Skipper, and we'll go hunting once Shades and Romeo have boots on the ground. Once they're down, retrieve the packs and see if you can raise Boss-man on the SAT phone."

"Copy that." Logan shoved their restrained prisoner in the direction of where Knight had said he had the girl secured. "Keep your mouth shut and move it, fucktard, and I don't advise making me shoot your ass—I'll enjoy it too fucking much."

A hand trailed up Ian's naked leg, and he smiled without opening his eyes. Cuddling his wife closer to his side, he asked, "Still feeling frisky, Angel?"

"Yes, Sir. Very frisky."

He let her close her hand around his growing cock and play for a bit. His brother had told him how horny Kristen had gotten during her pregnancy, and it appeared Angie was going to be the same way—thank God.

After waking up about an hour and a half ago, just before sunrise, he'd quietly stepped out of the room and checked in with the Sheriff's Department before passing on the intel to his team that Mallory Hart was still missing. The snowstorm they'd been worried about had decided to throw a wrench into the search. Ian wasn't worried about his team—dealing with the unexpected was part of their training—but the poor girl's chances of survival were dissipating. The helicopters would be grounded soon, but the search on foot, ATVs, and horseback would continue as long as possible. Ian planned on rejoining the search and rescue—he'd been out with the sheriff yesterday on ATVs for a few hours—but Angie was making it very difficult for him to leave her.

Upon returning to their room at the bed and breakfast after making his phone calls, he'd found his beautiful, naked woman kneeling in the center of their bed in full submissive position. Her head had been down with her hands resting on her knees, palms up. It had been the first time since her morning sickness had started weeks ago that she'd been up to playing first thing in the morning, and who was he to deny her?

Angie's gynecologist was familiar with the lifestyle and had given her a list of play that was and wasn't allowed. Ian had been pleasantly surprised to see a lot of his favorite things to do to his sub were in the allowed column. He'd gone easy on her this morning, though, ever mindful her nausea could come back with a vengeance. Instead of tying her to the bed and having his wicked way with her, he'd had her sit on his face while he had his preferred breakfast. The whole time— and it was a long time—she'd been instructed to play with those gorgeous tits of hers. After he'd made her come twice, he'd rolled her onto her back and taken her slowly and easily until she begged for more. Now it seemed as if his Angel was up for round two—and so was he.

Slowly, she pumped his cock as he pushed the covers off both of them. "As good as that feels, Angel, I know what would feel better."

"And what would that be, Master?"

Damn, he loved that seductive lilt in her voice. "Those luscious lips around my dick until it bounces off the back of your throat. Straddle me so I can play with that ass I love."

"Mmm. You read my mind. There's lube on the nightstand."

Ian's brow shot up as he glanced over and saw she was right. How the hell had he missed that earlier? He reached for it as one long leg crossed over his chest, and Angie settled on top of him, facing his feet. As he was admiring her bare pussy and heart-shaped ass, her mouth closed around him, and his eyes rolled back in his head. "Fuck, woman! I'll never get tired of you blowing me. Promise me when we're eighty, you'll still suck me whenever I ask you to."

Her chuckle vibrated around him before she lifted her head. "You never ask, Sir, you order. And, yes, when we're eighty, I'll still want you . . ." Her tongue licked his length and then the slit at the tip where a pearl of pre-cum had gathered. ". . . every long and delicious inch of you."

She was torturing him with her mouth—not that he minded at all—and he was more than willing to return the favor. With one hand, he squeezed her ass, and with the other, he flipped the top of the lubricant open and dripped some down the crack of her ass. Recapping the tube, he tossed it aside and spread her cheeks wide. Using his thumb, he worked the slick liquid into her back hole while the fingers of his other hand cupped her sex and teased her clit. Once she was well-lubed, he replaced his thumb with an index finger and pushed in slowly. At the same time, he parted her labia then entered her there too.

Angie gasped at the dual attack, and Ian felt it in his balls. As if knowing they tingled, she cupped and rolled them in her hand. Her tongue curved around his thick stalk before her cheeks hollowed and she sucked hard. Ian's eyes fluttered shut for a moment as he savored the sensations. "Time for a little game, Angel. If I make you come first, then you'll wear a vibrating plug on the jet ride home with me controlling it by remote any time I want. If you make me come first, you get to decide where we'll go on vacation next month."

Releasing him, she peeked over her shoulder at him, her eyes bright with lust and excitement. "Vacation? Like leave Tampa behind and head to a tropical island and act like tourists?"

"If that's what you want, yes." Honestly, it didn't matter where they went—as long as she was in his bed every night, they could be on the moon for all he cared. The Omega Team would officially be on their own, and with the addition of the Personal Protection Division at Trident, Ian and Devon were free to leave each other in charge of the zoo for a week or two. The West Coast Team would be coming to the Rockies next week, then the Sawyer brothers would have to fly out to San Diego for a few days to sit down with Jake Donovan and decide who was going to be the team leader. Jake had been running things from the startup of Trident Security West (TSW), but when his fiancé, Dev and Ian's youngest brother, Nick, opted out of the Navy in a few months, they'd be moving back to Tampa. "But shopping is limited to one hour per day."

"Deal." Wrapping her lips around his cock again, she repeatedly took him to the back of her throat as he sped up his assault on her pussy and ass. As they tortured each other with the intense passion always present when they were intimate, Ian knew no matter who won the bet, he'd still take her on a vacation next month. But that didn't mean he wasn't going to do his damnedest to get her to come first.

He used his fingers to fuck both her pussy and ass, while tapping her clit. He was relentless, yet so was she. Angie was extremely talented and dedicated when it came to blowjobs and loved giving them. Of course, he loved receiving them—what guy didn't?

Her head bobbed up and down as she slurped and moaned. Ian's body responded to the pleasure it was receiving and was barreling toward nirvana, but he wasn't losing this erotic battle. For lack of a third hand, he leaned forward and bit her ass cheek while pressing hard on her clit. Her walls rippled and clenched around his fingers as the orgasm overtook her and not a moment too soon. Ian bucked his hips upward, his tip touching the back of Angie's throat as he found his own release. She swallowed furiously, not letting a single drop escape.

As their heart rates and breathing returned to normal, his wife rolled off him, carefully lifting her leg, so she didn't accidentally kick him in the face. Snatching her ankle, he kissed the arch of her foot. "I love you, Angel."

Dropping onto her side, her tongue licked her lips. She stretched like a sated kitten. "Mmm, enough that I don't have to wear a vibrating plug and be at your mercy on the jet, Master?"

Resting her foot on his chest, he rubbed her lower leg. He grinned at her attempt to turn things around. "I love you enough to follow through on that, since you'll be begging me to fuck you when we finally make it back home. But . . ." His hand trailed up to her naked hip and back down again. "I'll make it up to you by letting you pick where you want to go on vacation. You and I and Little Bit can get away for two weeks before you can't travel anymore. When he or she comes into this world, we'll lose any chance of getting a full night's sleep for the next eighteen years, so let's take advantage of the time we have."

Angie let out an adorable snort. "You're being dramatic, Sir, but since I'm getting a first-class trip to St. Lucia out of it, be as dramatic as you want. Now, before you head out again to search for that girl, feed me, please."

"I thought I just did."

"Just because your sperm created Little Bit, doesn't mean it'll sustain him or her."

"Yes, dear." Laughing, Ian nibbled on her big toe. "St. Lucia, huh? Good choice."

As Cain scaled down the side of the cliff, Mancini was lowering the team's deployment bags next to him. Once Cain and the gear were down, the other man would join the party below. After securing the prisoner with Batman, Cowboy was at the tree line, covering his team-mates as they made their descent.

Once they caught the other three men, they'd find an area where a helicopter could land to take the prisoners and the girl back to civilization. The team would then finish their training run. They had all proven they worked well together, and Cain was looking forward to Omega being sent out on their own for future missions. He'd gotten used to going to work and getting dirty—it was a huge difference from his Secret Service suits and ties.

However, if the need arose for him to take the lead in a situation that required him to pull them out of the closet, he was all set. Blending into the background in a social setting, yet being close enough to his asset to protect them, was something he'd learned early on in his career in Washington D.C.—it wasn't as easy as people thought it was.

Glancing down before his next push off the wall, he noticed he was halfway there. Thank God he wasn't scared of heights. Another ten foot drop brought him that much closer to the ground. His feet made contact against the bluff a split second before something impacted the rock face next to him. A rifle report immediately followed. *Fuck!* Someone was shooting at him, and he was defenseless in this position. "I'm taking fire. Repeat, I'm taking fire. Not hit, but damn fucking close."

His co-leader's voice came over the comms. "Fuck! Drop fast and get the fuck out of there. Anyone have eyes on the shooter?" Had it not been an emergency, Cain might have snarked about that being an obvious thing to do, but McCabe was still issuing orders after there were no confirmed sightings. "Costello, find me that sniper. Batman, you've got the girl. Cowboy, as soon as Shades is down, join the search. Skipper, you're with me. Shot came from north of my location, one klick from the cliff. Romeo, you still got your rifle up there?"

"Affirmative."

"Drop the bags, make sure Shades is down, then get back to Costello. Find this bastard."

"Copy that."

Another shot echoed throughout the landscape, and it took Cain a second to register what the bullet had struck.

The *thunk* he'd heard had been one of their gear bags getting hit. At least it hadn't been him.

He pushed off the rock for a twenty foot drop as Mancini quickly lowered the bags to the ground. Flat out dropping them wasn't an option, since it might damage the SAT phone and some other equipment in them. Letting the rope slide through his glove-protected hands as fast as he could without killing himself, Cain rejoiced for all of a half a second when his feet touched the ground. He quickly undid his harness, pulled off his right glove with his teeth, and had his weapon in his hand in record time. "I'm down and with Cowboy."

Staying low, he headed for his teammate at the tree line. His adrenaline flowed as they joined the hunt. A thought flashed through his mind as they moved carefully from cover to cover—he wouldn't be surprised if Ian had prearranged this whole screwed-up rescue. The man had a twisted sense of humor at times. Had it not been for the real bullets flying, Cain would have entertained the thought a little longer as he kept watch for tangos. Fluffs of white fell from the sky in front of his face, and he rolled his eyes—fucking Boss-man definitely had to have planned this or, at least, wished it upon them. If he hadn't, then God had a warped sense of humor too.

Chapter Ten

Stalking stealthily through the woods, Tristan searched for their target. After the second shot, all had gone quiet. Thankfully, his co-leader had made it down without taking a bullet in the back. No one on the team had their bullet-proof vests on—who knew that one piece of equipment would be what they now wished they hadn't left behind? *Mental note—tell Boss-man to make sure TSW have theirs when they come to do this training run next week.*

The hair on the back of his neck stood up, and he brought his fist up to shoulder height, stopping Morrison in his tracks behind him. Tristan had long ago learned not to ignore the sixth sense both he and his brother, Emmett, had seemingly inherited from their father's side of the family. Their grandmother had called it their Celtic second sight. Whatever it was, Emmett swore it had saved his life many times during his Army tours in Afghanistan and Iraq, and since his older brother felt the same, Tristan never argued the fact.

Tristan's head swiveled as he searched for the reason his instincts were shouting at him. A single shot was fired, and a piece of bark from the tree he was using for cover went flying. It had missed him by centimeters. Ducking, he and Morrison squatted behind two trees and zeroed in on where the sniper was. The bastard was about thirty yards north of them. Using hand signals, Tristan told his teammate to make a distraction to their right, while he skirted around to the left and tried to pin the tango down.

Mindful of the fact there were two more suspects unaccounted for, he waited for Morrison to draw the sniper's fire. He didn't have to wait long. The former SWAT officer conjured up just enough noise by stepping on some twigs to divert the other man's attention. Another shot was fired in the general area Skipper was in as Tristan advanced from the other direction. His team-mate whispered a reassurance that he hadn't taken a hit.

Minuscule movement of a bush ahead and to the right had his gaze shifting. About fifteen yards away, the camouflaged man's attention was concentrated on Skipper's location. He was about thirty years old and could be the poster boy for the word redneck. Tristan expected him to spit tobacco through an open space in his teeth at any moment.

Raising his HK416 assault rifle, Tristan quietly got the asshole in his sights through the falling snowflakes, but a deer darted between them. At the sudden noise, the target spun back around and spotted the operative partially hidden by a tree. His gaze met Tristan's, and in a split second, he registered the fact he'd been deceived.

"Don't do it," Tristan muttered at the man even though he was too far away to hear. "Don't you fucking do it."

But the words went unheeded, and he had no option but to take the shot as the barrel of the redneck's rifle came around, aiming directly at him. The three-bullet burst from Tristan's weapon hit the man's center mass, and he went flying backward to the ground as his finger squeezed the trigger of his rifle. Tristan ducked, but the shot went wide and wild, thankfully not in the direction of any of his teammates. With any luck, the bastard shot one of his buddies.

It was at times like this, the former Delta Force lieutenant wished real life was like the movies. Hollywood made it look so easy to shoot a gun from a suspect's hands or aim for an arm or leg from any distance and have pinpoint accuracy. But everyone in the military and law enforcement had it drilled into them from day one of weapons training—aim for the center of the threat's chest and be prepared to kill. If it's a choice between you or the bad guy going home alive at the end of the day, that was the best way to ensure you came out on top.

The echoed report of his weapon firing faded away, and there was a short moment of silence before the usual sounds of the forest resumed. This wasn't a glamorous movie set, and it was highly unlikely the suspect was still breathing, but Tristan wasn't taking chances until it was confirmed. As he approached, weapon still at the ready, Morrison moved in from the other direction, also prepared to shoot if necessary. When they reached the man, he was flat on his back, blood covered his chest and seeped out of the large wounds that had to be on his back, mixing with the brown earth and white snow around him. His unseeing eyes were wide open, staring at the tops of the pine trees above. Even though it was evident the man was dead, Skipper still kicked the rifle away from the body, then squatted down to check for a pulse in the man's neck as Tristan covered him.

Shaking his head, Morrison stood again. "Tango Two is down and out," he announced quietly into his comm microphone. "Any sign of Three or Four?"

One by one, Knight, Abbott, Mancini, Reese, and Foster all responded, "Negative."

Twenty minutes later, they rendezvoused with the rest of the team after Abbott and Mancini finally came down from the bluff. They hadn't spotted the third brother nor the father, so it was time to call in the local law for reinforcements. The US Marshals and FBI would be getting involved once it was confirmed the men were the ones who'd robbed the bank and killed the guard and police officer. They could finish the hunt while the Omega team returned the girl to her family, then headed back to civilization themselves.

Tristan and Morrison found the others had retrieved the deployment bags as they were the last to return. Grabbing his bag, Tristan opened it, pulled out the sat phone, and cursed. He held it up for the others to see. "We're not out of this yet, boys and girls. That bastard shot up our only communications with the outside world."

"Damn." Reese held out his hand. "Let me take a look. Maybe I can salvage it." He'd been the communications specialist on his MARSOC team, so if anyone could fix the thing, it was him. But after a brief assessment, all he did was hand it back to Tristan. "If I had my tools, I might've been able to repair it enough to get a signal out, but since I don't, we're shit out of luck. So much for calling in the troops, unless one of these assholes or the girl have a cell phone."

Reese hadn't discovered a phone on their prisoner during the earlier search for weapons. Morrison had patted the dead man's clothing, before leaving him where he fell, and had found no cell, but had removed a pistol from his belt holster and retrieved his rifle. When Darius asked Mallory, she reported her SAT phone had been destroyed by the men.

Shit. With no way to communicate with Ian or the local law, they had to finish this lovely stroll through the wilderness with their prisoner, who was refusing to talk beyond the occasional "fuck off," and Mallory in tow. The snow continued to fall, sticking to everything it landed on, and it was getting heavier every minute. To top it all off, they had no idea where the other two suspects were. *Well, shit and fuck.*

Tristan eyed the young woman who was staying close to Batman while glaring at the man she'd identified as Darrell. While she denied being hurt, she wasn't dressed for the colder temperatures which had been dropping for the past two hours. In fact, her lips were turning blue. He knew when the other men had a moment, after assuring there was no immediate threat, one of them would be offering up his heavier jacket for her to wear—might as well be him.

As the others stood guard, he pulled Mancini, Morrison, and Foster aside for a moment. Addressing the first two men, he said, "Go get the camo jacket off our dead guy. He was about my size. I'll wear it and give mine to the girl—she's already feeling the cold. Depending on how long this snow lasts, we might have to make camp and a fire sooner than expected to keep her warm. Mark where we're leaving the body so the sheriff's department can retrieve it. Hopefully the snow will keep it from becoming dinner for any animals, but that's the least of our problems right now."

As they took off to follow his orders, he removed his jacket and turned to their new asset. He'd heard the others introduce themselves to her earlier through his earpiece. "Hi, Mallory, my name's Tristan McCabe. Put this on over your coat—it looks like the temps are going to keep dropping." She shook her head, and he stopped what was sure to be a protest from spilling from her lips. "It's fine. My men will be back in a few minutes with another jacket for me." While she wouldn't miss the blood on his replacement jacket, she didn't need to know in advance where it was coming from.

Taking it from him, she gave him a grateful smile as she put it on. With the size difference between him and her, it swallowed her. At least it would keep her warm. "Hi. Thanks for this. And like I told your teammates, thanks for rescuing me."

"No thanks are necessary. But I do have a few questions for you. Do you have any idea which direction you came from, and how far you've come from where they grabbed you?" he asked as Foster stepped over, unfolding the map they'd brought along. If this had been a real mission, they would have had an extra sat phone as well as a tablet or laptop with GPS capabilities. But Boss-man had limited their gear, so they had to work together, using all their training to get to their intended destination.

While Foster held the map for her to see, Mallory studied it a moment, then pointed at a spot. She'd had to push the sleeve of his jacket up to get her finger out. "This is Lower Blue Lake where I ran into them. The lot where I parked my car is about two miles north of that. I know we went east for about two or three hours before we made camp. Then yesterday, we hiked for several hours—southeast, I think—but I have no idea how far."

"You covered quite a bit of distance since then." McCabe ran his finger up from where she'd indicated the men had taken her to their current location southwest of there. "This is where we are now, just below Potosi Peak." It was basically a lopsided triangle, with approximately the same distance to get to either where she'd left her car or the town of Ouray. Since heading the way she'd come increased their chances of running into the other two suspects, it was best they continued on their planned route. While there would be some obstacles, they didn't have to rappel any more cliffs. But they would be spending one more night out here unless they managed to make contact with the outside world.

Morrison and Mancini returned, and the latter handed him the red-stained jacket with a bullet hole in the front and an even larger exit hole in the back. Mallory's eyes widened as he put on the garment. "Th-that was the last gunshot we heard?"

Darrell stared at Tristan in confusion for a moment before the blood registered. "You bastard! You killed my brother! Jessup! Jessup!" With his hands at his lower back, he struggled to get to his knees, but Foster prevented him from standing. "You fucking bastards! You'll fucking pay for this! If it's the last fucking thing I do, I'm going to kill all of you! You hear me? All of you!"

During Darrell's rant, Morrison had reached into his

deployment bag's outside pocket and pulled out a roll of silver duct tape. Ripping off a strip, he slapped it across their prisoner's mouth. With his other brother and father still out there, they didn't need him announcing their movements.

Mallory glanced in the direction Morrison and Mancini had come from moments before. "Did he have a scar on his cheek?" she asked quietly to no one in particular.

"Yes," Tristan responded.

"Good. I hope he saw the bullet coming, the bastard. He's the one who couldn't wait to rape me."

Knight cupped her chin and gently forced her to look at him. His voice was tender as he told her, "He's dead, and we'll keep you safe. The others won't get to you, because they'll never get past us first. Understood?"

A tear of relief rolled down her cheek, but she quickly brushed it away, before squaring her shoulders and standing straighter. "I know I keep saying it, but thank you. I told you my dad's a retired Marine—he taught me how to survive out here and how to follow orders in emergencies. I won't slow you down, and if you say jump, I'll ask how high."

Grins spread across the faces of Omega Team, and Lindsey stepped over to the younger woman who had shown more strength in that one declaration than most people her age had shown in their whole lives. The sniper jerked a thumb toward Reese who was keeping his gaze on the woods to her left. "Cowboy and I are both Marine Corps too. Stick with him and me, and we'll show the grunts, frog, and secret agent man over there how we get things done. *Oohrah.*"

Tristan chuckled as he grabbed his deployment bag. "Just don't forget the frog is the one who'll be dishing out the shit details on this mission. We've got a lot of ground to cover, and the snow is going to slow us down even more. Batman and Shades, you've got the asset. Romeo, you're with me on the redneck. Let's move out."

His teammates knew what he hadn't verbalized—keep their eyes peeled for the other two tangos. Batman had told Mallory the truth in cold, hard facts—those bastards weren't going to lay a hand on her again. Not while Omega Team was guarding her.

TRUDGING BEHIND HIS FATHER, BILLY RAY TRIED TO FIGURE out how to convince him they were going in the wrong direction. Nothing he'd said earlier had worked. When Jessup woke up, he'd been so furious the girl had gotten away that he'd smacked his youngest brother across the face. Billy Ray had clenched his sore jaw and fists while the bastard had screamed at him—as if it were his fault Susan had gotten away. Well, actually it had been, but he'd never admit it.

It would've been futile to fight back, since he always lost quickly against Jessup or Darrell. They were a lot bigger and stronger than he was . . . and apparently smarter since it hadn't taken them long to figure out the direction Susan had taken. She'd been easy to track at first, but then she'd managed to throw them off a few times, giving her a little extra time to evade them.

Ross and Darrell had been just as pissed when they'd returned to camp at the same time as the other two. Grabbing their gear and rifles, they'd quickly set out after her. From what Billy Ray figured, she'd had about a half hour head start on them. But as Darrell and Jessup went east, directly after her, Ross had ordered his youngest to stay with him as he headed more east than south. They knew once she reached the river, a few miles away, she'd follow it back to civilization like Billy Ray had told her to. He was doing his best to slow his father down, but it wasn't working. It just got him yelled at some more, and he knew they were closing in on her again. A few times in the last ten minutes, he'd heard Jessup taunting her.

As much as he wanted to see her again, he didn't want his brothers and father to rape and kill her. She was too nice and pretty for them to do that to her. While they'd hiked to the second camp yesterday, she'd talked to him as if they were friends, telling him about her family, school, and photography. They'd tried to keep their voices low, so his father wouldn't tell them to shut up again.

She had a sweet smile, and it reminded him of his mother. What Lara Greenly had seen in her husband, Billy Ray didn't know, but he may not have existed if she hadn't loved the man. His mother had died of pneumonia when he was nine years old. All he had left of her was a couple of pictures he'd taken from the garbage after his father had thrown them out in a drunken rage one night.

"God damn it, Billy Ray," Ross hissed. "You got lead fucking feet? Fucking move it. We lose that girl, and she'll tell fucking everyone we're out here. I'm not going to fucking jail because of some dumb bitch."

"Yes, Pa."

He took three, maybe four, more steps when a single rifle shot pierced the air. Billy Ray and Ross froze, and moments later another shot resounded, followed by silence.

"Dumb shits!" Ross whispered harshly. "What the fuck are they shooting at? I'll kick their fucking asses."

Billy Ray didn't answer. Anything he said would surely have the man's ire turning on him. He'd learned over the years it was best to remain silent when his father was pissed.

From the sound of it, they were approximately a mile north of wherever the shots had been fired, and Ross hurried south with his youngest son on his heels. Billy Ray prayed his brothers hadn't killed Susan. Maybe it was a bear or cougar they'd shot at. God, he hoped so.

The gray clouds finally released their soft, white flakes which floated down to the ground. Billy Ray inwardly cursed. When the snow started to stick and then thicken, it would be even easier to track Susan. He was also worried she'd freeze with the drop in temperatures. She hadn't been dressed for the colder weather which had moved in after several warmer days.

Following his father, he racked his brains, trying to come up with a way to help her escape, but everything he visualized would wind up with him getting his ass kicked. *Fuck.*

CHAPTER ELEVEN

The snow was getting deeper, but they would keep moving until they absolutely had to stop and make camp. If they were lucky, they might be able to find a natural shelter somewhere so they could dry off by a fire.

Reese, Foster, and Darius were guarding their prisoner and Mallory during their trek east, while McCabe and Abbott were a klick to their north, and Morrison and Mancini hiked a klick to the south. They'd spread out to see if they could spot the other two men still out there somewhere—they had to be cautious of an ambush.

Darius had to hand it to the young woman—she was a hell of a trooper. He wondered if she'd ever thought of enlisting in the armed forces because she had the smarts and gumption for it. Never once had she complained about the hike, the snow, or the cold. After Duracell had given her his jacket to wear, Darius had removed his knit cap and placed it on her head. The team had needed to keep their gloves on—in a high-risk situation, having your trigger finger numb from the cold was not a good thing—so Costello had dug out an extra pair of socks she'd stuffed into her deployment bag. Mallory now looked like a homeless bag lady with the wool socks covering her hands, the oversized jacket she was almost drowning in, and her wet, blonde hair sticking out of the cap.

They had a few instant heat packs between them, but they were saving them in case of an emergency. Right now, they were a luxury they couldn't afford to waste. They might be out here longer than expected and they had to conserve their resources. They had enough MREs to feed everyone tonight, but they'd be sharing the remainders in the morning. Darius was tempted to feed their prisoner the one cheese omelet meal he'd spotted in their stash and let the man suffer for the rest of the hike to Ouray. Lord knew the rest of them weren't going to eat it.

As the snow continued to fall, they stayed under the trees as much as possible. The wind wasn't blowing too much at the moment, and the canopy of pine branches high above them prevented the snow from building up too fast around the tree trunks. In the three hours since the storm had settled overhead, about four to five inches had been dumped on them.

Directly in front of Darius, their prisoner—Mallory had told them his name was Darrell—tripped on a snow-covered root or rock and pitched forward. Reese's hand shot out and grabbed the man's arm before he fell to the ground. With his wrists still restrained, they couldn't have him breaking something in a fall. No one wanted to carry his sorry ass if came down to it.

"Darius?"

"Yeah, Mal, what's wrong?" They'd been chatting in

low voices for the better part of their journey about a variety of things, and it'd felt natural to shorten her name in conversation. She hadn't objected to it, so he assumed it was a nickname she'd been called by her family and friends.

"Nothing's wrong." Even though her cheeks were red from the cold, he could tell she was blushing. "I just really need to pee again."

That wasn't a surprise. She'd been a little dehydrated when he'd found her and had drank quite a bit of water from his supply. Replenishing it wouldn't be a problem between the snow and the river Romeo and Morrison were walking near.

"Guys, hold up," he called out to Cowboy and Shades who came to a halt a few feet ahead of them. "We need a quick pit stop." Glancing around, he pointed to a nearby thicket just past a large, downed tree. "That should give you enough coverage. We'll wait here. Keep your eyes and ears open."

"I will. Thanks." She hurried over to where he'd indicated and skirted around the huge root ball that had been yanked from the earth when the nearly hundred-foot-tall pine tree had fallen at some point in the not so recent past.

"I gotta piss too," their prisoner whined. They'd ripped the tape off his mouth earlier when his breathing got heavier from the highs and lows of the hike. However, they'd warned him it would be no skin off their backs to slap it back on if he didn't stay quiet.

While Foster aimed his weapon at Darrell, Reese pulled out the blade of his Leatherman tool. "Turn around, and remember we've got no problem shooting your ass if you try to run. Make it fast." He cut the plastic tie, freeing the man's hands, then reached into the pocket of his cargo pants where he had several more zip ties and pulled one out.

The sounds of the forest around them had been muted by the snowfall. Darius glanced around. He estimated the remaining distance to the outskirts of Ouray would take about four hours to cover, maybe five with the snow slowing them down. With the sun above the thick layer of clouds, darkness was approaching earlier than it had yesterday. They'd have to start looking for a place to bed down for the night.

When Darrell zipped his fly back up, Reese restrained his wrists again. A soft, indistinguishable sound reached Darius's ears. His eyes narrowed, and his gaze returned to the fallen tree as he tried to figure out what he'd heard. "Mallory? You okay?"

She didn't answer him, and the three operatives immediately went on alert. Reese automatically shoved their prisoner to the ground, so he wouldn't be a distraction or try to run away. Darius took several tentative steps toward where she'd disappeared behind the flora. "Mal?"

From the thicket, a man stood from a crouch holding a 9mm pistol to Mallory's temple with his other hand around her throat, holding her in place. Dressed in camouflage, he'd blended in with the surroundings. Appearing older than their prisoner and the man they'd killed, he had to be their father.

Darius cursed inwardly. How the hell had the bastard gotten close enough to grab her without them hearing or seeing him? It was a thought he pushed aside—now was not the time to analyze how they got to this point. The three Omega teammates had their weapons trained on what little of the man wasn't being blocked by Mallory. There were too many factors preventing them from shooting him without risking her getting hit as well. *Where the hell is the other brother?*

As if answering Darius's unspoken question, a kid barely out of his teens stepped out from behind a tree to the right of his father, his rifle aimed at Reese, who had one boot on Darrell's back. Their father glared at his opponents. "Let my boy go or I'll fucking kill her right here."

Yeah, neither of those things were going to happen if they had anything to say about it. Standing between Reese and Darius, Foster had shifted his weapon and was aiming it at the kid, as the other two kept the older man in their sights. Darius took a few steps to his right, trying to find a better angle in case he had to shoot. He did his best to ignore the terror in Mallory's eyes. "You know how this goes—you shoot her and we shoot you."

"You assholes won't let me shoot her and you know it. Darrell, get your ass up."

Reese put more of his weight on the prisoner's back, eliciting a string of curses and some struggling. "Stay put, Darrell, or I'll blow out the back of both your knees."

They were in a Mexican standoff—a stalemate where neither party had the advantage until something happened to tilt it in one direction. There was no way to alert the rest of Omega without giving away the fact they were out there. Darius had no idea if these men knew four more operatives were with them, but at the moment, it didn't matter since they were a good distance away to the north and south.

"Where's Jessup?" the older man spat.

"They killed him, Pa! They fucking murdered him!" Darrell shouted before Reese pushed the air out of his lungs.

The hand around Mallory's neck tightened as the man's angry expression turned thunderous. He waved the gun in their direction, pointing it at one and then the other, then back again. "You fucking bastards! I'll fucking kill you all! Darrell, get your ass up!"

The youngest son's head zipped back and forth between all the parties involved. Darius was surprised to see he appeared to be as afraid of what his father might do to Mallory as he was of the men he was confronting. She'd told the team how one of the men had let her escape, and it wasn't hard to figure out it was him. His rifle wasn't aimed at anyone in particular anymore. Instead, it was pointed downward, and if fired, the bullet would hit the snow-covered dirt a few feet in front of Foster.

Darius took a chance and looked Mallory in the eye, willing her to be courageous enough to give them a hand in saving her. He saw the moment she drew strength from his stare and blinked three times in rapid succession, acknowledging her understanding of his unspoken command. They needed a diversion, a split second distraction to get her out of harm's way, so the team could take their shots, and she was about to give it to them. Darius hoped like hell it worked.

As the father yelled more demands, Mallory pulled the socks off her hands and dropped them in the snow. Darius took careful aim as she threw her hands up and back, scratching and clawing at the guy's face. Several things happened at once and seemed to move in slow motion. The man cursed and shoved her straight out and away from him, causing her to remain in the line of fire. He brought his gun hand up as Darius shifted for a better shot. Foster dove for Mallory, knocking her down and covering her with his body.

The kid . . . Jesus, the kid did something completely unexpected. He lunged in front of his father's weapon to protect Mallory. "No! Don't—"

But the bastard had already begun to pull the trigger and didn't stop. The gun discharged, and the kid's body jolted when the round struck his chest, throwing him to the ground. Finally having clear shots, Reese and Darius opened fire, riddling the older man with bullets until he was no longer a threat. His body danced as it absorbed the impacts before falling at the base of a tree. The reports from the weapons echoed then faded around them as everything returned to normal speed in Darius's mind.

Foster rolled off Mallory and immediately checked her for any sign of being hit. Darius rushed over and kicked the pistol out of the dead man's hand as a precaution, and then did the same to the rifle lying next to the kid.

Turning his weapon back to Darrell, who was once again struggling to get out from under the boot holding him down, Reese barked, "Don't fucking move, asshole."

Sitting up, Mallory assured Foster she wasn't injured, then cried out when she spotted the young man who was covered in blood and gasping for air a few feet away from her. She scrambled over as Darius dropped to his knees in the snow and ripped open the kid's coat, so he could try and stop the bleeding. Mallory grabbed the injured man's hand. "Billy Ray! Oh, God, help him, Darius! He's the one that let me escape. Billy Ray, you're going to be okay. You saved my life."

Billy Ray's pain-filled gaze fell onto Mallory's face. He swallowed hard twice before attempting to speak. "Are . . . are you o-okay, Su-Susan?"

Yanking the emergency kit from his deployment bag, Foster quickly found the trauma dressings and ripped the package open as Darius used his knife to cut Billy Ray's shirt. Reaching out, Mallory wiped the snow from the injured man's face. "Yes. I'm fine, thanks to you. And I lied —my name's not Susan. It's Mallory."

His relief was evident as he struggled to breathe. He was dying, and there was nothing the others could do about it. "M-Mallory . . . I like—like that name. Pretty." His gaze searched hers, possibly looking for forgiveness. "I-I'm so-sorry."

Having heard the shots, the rest of the team came running from opposite directions and slowed as they took in the bloody scene before them. After assuring themselves none of their teammates or Mallory had been shot, they hurried to help the others anyway they could.

"*Sh.* It's okay. Don't talk. You're going to be fine," Mallory promised Billy Ray in a soft voice. A quick glimpse told Darius Mallory didn't believe her own words, but she repeated them anyway for comfort. "You're going to be just fine."

Her gaze flickered to where Darius's hands were applying pressure to the wound covered by a thick, white dressing, before returning to the dying man's face. She gently stroked his forehead. "I would've been honored to be your girlfriend."

Billy Ray Greenly died with a small smile accompanying a look of awe on his face. Tears rolled down Mallory's cheeks as she continued to stroke his brow after he'd taken his last breath then stilled. Once again, silence filled the air. Darkness would be upon them soon as the sun began to set behind the clouds.

Shaking his head at the senseless bloodshed, Darius got to his feet. He gave Mallory a few more moments to grieve the death of her unexpected savior, then extended his hand to help her up. "Come on, Mal. We have to find shelter for the night. I promise we'll send a recovery team out for him when we get to Ouray."

Accepting his hand, she stood. With a final glance at Billy Ray, she turned and walked away.

WITH CC IN THE CO-PILOT SEAT, BABS LIFTED THE Blackhawk off the ground with frustration just after 8:00 a.m. There had been no sign of the missing girl, nor word from Omega. Ian had lost contact with them after an update with them early yesterday morning. Since then, he'd been trying to get ahold of them via the SAT phone, after the snow had started, with no success. Back in Tampa, Nathan had assured their boss the satellite needed for the team's connection was working properly and in the right position for them to receive calls. They just weren't answering. It was either turned off, had malfunctioned, or something far worse had happened. She just prayed it wasn't the latter.

Yesterday around noon, the snowstorm had finally forced Babs and the pilots of the two SAR helicopters to return to the small airport. They'd managed to stay in the air for about ninety minutes after the flakes had started falling. Even though they were on the northern edge of the storm, the increasing snowfall and wind had made for poor visibility, grounding the helicopters for its duration. Having been on many search and rescue missions and troop extractions over the years, she'd hated leaving a team out there on their own without communications, especially in a storm. She knew the men and one woman on Omega could handle themselves in any situation—they wouldn't have been hired by the Sawyer brothers if they couldn't—but she still had a bad feeling about whatever was happening on that mountain.

"TS-actual, this is TS-one-five," Babs voiced into her headset's microphone. "We're up and heading for the route Omega should be on."

"TS-actual copies. Bring those idiots home." Despite Ian's growled, derogatory response, she knew he was worried about the team too, even though he had full confidence in them.

After she'd gained altitude and banked the aircraft to the west, the two SAR helicopters took off as well. They'd be heading northwest trying to locate the missing girl, while Babs and CC were en route to Omega's last known location. From there, they'd follow the route the team was supposed to be taking back to Ouray. If they heard the Blackhawk buzzing overhead, they'd most likely know she was searching for them, since there'd be no other reason for the military-grade bird to be in that area. They'd find a way to signal her somehow.

With their camouflage tactical clothing, it would be hard to spot them among the green and brown landscape, even with the snow on the ground, unless they were out in the open. As for Mallory Hart, she'd reportedly been wearing a red coat, which should make her easier to find, but that depended on a lot of different circumstances. Was she just lost? Injured or sick? Did she want to be found? Or had something sinister happened to her?

Checking the coordinates on the instrument panel, Babs adjusted the helicopter's trajectory. Beside her, CC consulted the map he had on a tablet Ian had given him, and then pointed to a cliff. "According to Boss-man, that's the rock they had to scale down. They should have camped about a mile or so west of there."

Since they didn't know if the team ever made it to the bluff, Babs decided to check the campsite first. Once they verified there was no one in sight, she reversed direction and headed east, while CC scoured the landscape below with his binoculars. Babs called out every time she saw a heat signature that was large enough to be a person on a screen in the instrument panel, but each time, CC confirmed it was an animal.

For approximately fifteen minutes, they continued, in a grid pattern, north to south and then back again as they made their way east. Suddenly her co-pilot shouted, "Hey! Over there! Ten o'clock!"

Babs whipped her gaze to the left and then let out a relieved sigh. There was their team, standing in a small clearing about three and a half miles west of Ouray. They waved at her, and she briefly waggled the chopper from side to side to indicate she'd spotted them. It was too small an area for her to try to land, but she could still get close enough for a better assessment of the group. There were nine people, and standing between Abbott and Knight was a young woman wearing someone's camo jacket. She could only be the missing hiker out there in the middle of nowhere. After another quick head count, Babs realized there was an extra male among them too. Hovering overhead, she could see his hands were restrained behind his back.

Flipping a switch to activate the speaker system on the underside of the aircraft, she announced, "Glad to see you! Anyone hurt?"

Several of the team members gave her a negative signal as CC gave her the coordinates for a larger clearing about a mile southeast she could use as a landing zone. She relayed the information to the team, and after they acknowledged her, she pitched the bird in that direction. "TS-one-five to TS-one-actual. We found them, and it looks like they have the missing girl and one restrained tango with them." She rattled off the longitude and latitude of the team's location. "They're heading for an LZ about one and a half klicks south of that. We'll be bringing them home."

"TS-one-actual to TS-one-five, copy that. Any injuries?"

"None reported but will update when we have them on board."

"Copy that, and good job."

With the snow, it took the rag-tag group about twenty-five minutes to navigate the rocky terrain, and Babs had the helicopter on the ground waiting for them. She grinned at them as one by one they climbed aboard. Each one was dirtier than the last. "Just so you know, Boss-man said you failed, and you'll have to do the training run again," she teased. "You're coming back up here in two weeks with fifty pound packs this time."

"Fuck that shit," Mancini retorted as he helped the girl into the bird. "If we do, he can come with us to make sure we stay on target."

After getting the restrained man into the helicopter, McCabe was the last one to board, and Babs did a double take over her shoulder at the jacket he was wearing. It was covered in blood. It was then she noticed some of the others had blood on their hands and clothing, mixed in with the dirt. Lifting her gaze to McCabe's, she took in his grim expression, but all he said was, "Let's go, Babs. And do us a favor and leave out the roller coaster ride this time."

"Roger that. Buckle up, boys and girls. Let's get you home."

Chapter Twelve

Ian paced back and forth in the snow and slush at the small airport. The runway and helipads had already been plowed this morning, and one of the latter was currently empty, waiting for the Blackhawk to return. The two SAR helicopters had landed a few minutes ago after the pilots had been alerted the missing girl had been rescued. Even though Foster had called him from the bird, assuring him everyone was safe and sound, he still needed to see it with his own eyes. Abbott, Foster, Knight, Mancini, McCabe, Morrison, and Reese had not only become his employees, they'd become part of his extended family. And like every patriarch, he'd worry every time they went out on a mission until they all returned in one piece—not that he'd let them know that.

An ambulance idled nearby. The EMTs had been sent to evaluate Mallory Hart for any injuries or effects of exposure to the elements she may have incurred during her ordeal. They'd probably transport her to the hospital as a precaution. Her parents also anxiously awaited their daughter's return along with their three sons, her boyfriend, the sheriff, several SAR team members, and a few friends.

Angie sat in the passenger seat of the SUV Ian had driven to the airstrip, with the heat on high. He hadn't wanted her standing in the cold with the rest of them, but she'd insisted on accompanying him to see for herself the team was safe. She loved the new additions to the Trident family as much as she loved the original team members, and being pregnant had her in nesting mode. She needed to make sure all her ducklings were in a row before she could relax again.

Back at the gated entrance to the property, the sheriff's deputies were keeping the press at bay. After Mallory had been missing over a day, the local newspapers and TV networks had picked up the story. The number of reporters had doubled after another twenty-four hours with no sign of the vanished hiker. It wouldn't be long before they discovered her disappearance was related to the manhunt for three brothers and their father who'd robbed a bank and killed two people thirty miles away, as Foster had reported. When that happened, it would be a free-for-all to scoop the other reporters. The last thing Ian needed was to have his team's pictures splashed all over the internet, TV, and print editions—it would seriously fuck with their ability to work any covert ops.

The unmistakable thumping of the military-grade helicopter started low and slowly increased. Ian scanned the sky, trying to spot it since the precipitous topography of the surrounding area made it sound like it was coming from every direction.

The sheriff approached and pointed to Ian's right. Sure

enough, there was the big, black bird heading straight for them. With Babs at the controls, it flew into range, then like a majestic eagle, landed gently on its assigned helipad. As the rotors slowed, McCabe slid open the side door and stepped down. He turned and grabbed the arm of the one Greenly family member who hadn't been killed and pulled him down onto the tarmac. Two deputies stepped forward and took him into custody.

Reese was out the door next, followed by Knight, who helped their rescued charge down from the helicopter's bay. With a hand gesture to keep her head low until they cleared the reach of the overhead blades that were still moving, he hurried the young woman into her waiting family's arms. Her parents embraced her with such relieved emotion, Ian knew it would be quite a while before they let her out of their sight again.

As the rotors slowed to a stop and Babs shut down the engines, the rest of the exhausted team poured out of the aircraft, carrying their deployment bags and gear. They strode over to Ian who introduced each of them to Sheriff Collins. After a round of handshakes, backslaps, and thanks, Reese handed the lawman the rifles recovered from the Greenly men as McCabe placed two small canvas bags on the hood of the nearest patrol car with a clunk. "One of these has three 9mm and two .380s in it. The safeties are engaged, but other than that, we didn't mess with them. Figured for forensics and evidence, you'd need them as intact as possible with minimal handling. The other bag is knives, IDs, and a few other things we took off the bodies in case any animals decide they're hungry."

Mancini held out a piece of paper to Collins. "Here are

the coordinates of where the three bodies are located. One is near that second cliff we scaled, and the others are together a few miles south of there. We marked some trees with red and white locator paint." The aerosol cans were no bigger than a travel-size hairspray and easily fit in with their regular gear. They were great to mark a trail with, if needed, or in this case, the locations of dead bodies.

The sheriff nodded and waved over two of his deputies to take possession of the weapons. "I appreciate that. I'll also need whichever weapons of yours that were fired and a rundown of who took what shot for the investigation. I'll get the guns back to you as soon as we close the case. Unfortunately, that'll probably be a few weeks."

Foster snorted. "If we can go someplace warm so we can thaw out our balls, we'll go through a whole debrief."

Beside him, Abbot grinned. "Well, I don't have physical balls, but my metaphorical ones could definitely use a hot coffee and an even hotter shower."

"Let's head back to my office," Collins replied. "I can supply the coffee, but the showers will have to wait until we get your reports on paper. We'll try to get you in and out of there without the press getting any photos. I'll tell Mallory she's got to keep your identities a secret. She's a good kid, and I trust she'll keep quiet."

Before they had a chance to load up into Babs's and Ian's vehicles, Mallory rushed over to them. She had a white blanket from the ambulance around her shoulders, and McCabe's jacket in her hands. As her parents stood at her side, she held the jacket out to its owner who'd turned around to face her. "Thanks so much, Tristan. I'm sure you want to get out of that other one."

The big man glanced down at his chest as if he'd forgotten he had a dead man's coat on. Noting the three large, exit holes on the back, which were covered in blood, Ian couldn't wait to hear the entire story.

With a wry grin, Tristan removed the garment and gave it to the sheriff as evidence. Before he took his own jacket back, he bent down and gave Mallory a brotherly kiss on the cheek. Her smile grew as one by one, the Omega team said their goodbyes to her with either a hug or a kiss or both. With her going to the hospital, and the teammates going to give their official accounts of what happened before heading to the larger airport where their jet was waiting for them, they probably wouldn't see each other again. As her parents expressed their gratitude to the operatives, Mallory thanked each one and said goodbye. "I'm going to miss all of you. I don't know how I'll ever be able to thank you enough."

When it was the last man's turn to say goodbye, Darius held out his hand to her father first. "Mr. and Mrs. Hart? You've raised an incredible daughter. If it wasn't for her courage and the training you'd given her over the years, things would probably have turned out a lot differently. I'm sure it doesn't have to be said, but you should be damn proud of her."

Her parents agreed with him and, once again, expressed their thanks. Turning to the young woman, he handed her a piece of paper he'd quickly jotted something down on. "Here's my cell number and email—if you ever need anything, or get down to Florida for anything, give me a call."

The statement was spoken in a way that didn't allow any misinterpretation—the two had obviously developed a brother/sister relationship out in the wilderness. Ian knew if the girl ever did need anything, Knight would make sure he was there to help in any way he could.

Mallory stepped forward and wrapped her arms around his waist, her head resting on his massive chest. The corners of his mouth ticked upward as he returned the embrace. After a moment, she leaned back so she could see his face, which was still covered in grime. Her soft words were reminiscent of a line from *The Wizard of Oz* when she said, "I think I'll miss you most of all, Batman."

GLANCING UP FROM HER SKETCH, ANGIE SMILED AT THE bodies strewn about the jet's cabin. The team was exhausted. Ian had wanted to leave for the airport as soon as everyone had taken a quick shower, however, Mallory's family had insisted on treating everyone from Trident to lunch. They had to head back to Tampa and wouldn't be there tomorrow when her parents were throwing a thank you luncheon for everyone involved in the search and rescue at the American Legion hall.

Even Angie's husband was sacked out in one of the recliners, catching up on some much needed sleep. He'd been so tired, he'd forgotten the anal plug he'd wanted her to wear for the flight, and there was no way she was reminding him of the fact. She was sure he'd remember soon enough.

She wished they could go on their vacation tomorrow because he'd earned some relaxation time, but there were a few cases and missions coming up that required his attention. However, there was no stopping her from planning a getaway for them for next month. She was holding him to his promise, not only for herself, but for him. She loved taking care of her Dom as much as he loved taking care of her.

Studying the photo taped to the edge of her pad, she added a few more details to the sketch of Russell Adams and his dog, Jagger. The young Navy veteran was Trident's new assistant mechanic, who'd helped save Brody's life. The sketch was going to be a birthday present for him from Tori Freyja, one of the submissives from the club and the woman who'd trained Russell's PTSD service dog.

After seeing the half-finished sketch earlier, Babs had given Angie an idea. There were a few photographers across the US who had been aiding veteran amputees to find the beauty in their bodies once again. Seeing the professional photos being appreciated by the public was helping them heal and get their self-confidence back. The veterans rehab hospital in Tampa, where Babs went for therapy and adjustments to her prosthesis, had volunteers involved in different programs. Angie wasn't the greatest photographer in the world, but she got by enough for the photos needed for her graphic design business. Her artistic talent leaned more toward painting and sketching, and that's how she decided to honor any veteran who was willing to pose for her. After taking photos of them to work from and then using paint, she'd turn their bodies into works of art that would show the world the strength and vitality that still existed within them.

Ian and Devon had been talking about having their friend Parker erect a small building on the Trident property where both Angie and Devon's wife, Kristen, could spend their days getting creative. Kristen was a popular romance author, and Angie had even designed a few of her book covers. They would each have their own space, and so would their children. JD was just about six months old and would have a new cousin when Little Bit was finally born. Angie was looking forward to having a studio with more light to work with. Ian had agreed the building could have lots of windows as long as they were bulletproof. With the security business and its governmental contracts, the man wasn't taking any chances with his family's safety.

On the other side of the jet, Reese stood and stumbled to the bathroom, still half asleep. He was a man Angie was dying to sketch. She'd heard part of what he'd gone through over in Afghanistan, with minimal details, and her heart ached for him. While he seemed to be doing well physically, there was a darkness in his eyes that worried her. As far as she knew, he hadn't dated anyone since moving to Tampa, and her mind went through the list of her single friends not in the BDSM lifestyle, searching for someone she could hook him up with. Everyone deserved to find their soulmate—Angie had been lucky enough to find hers—and she wanted all of the extended Trident family to be as happily in love as she was.

A little jingle filled the air of the cabin, and it took Angie a moment to realize two things. One—it was Ernie from *Sesame Street* singing "Rubber Ducky." And two—it was coming from Ian's cell phone sitting on a small table next to him. Instantly awake, his eyes flew open as he grabbed the offensive device. "Fucking Brody. I'm going to kill him. I swear, one of these fucking days, I'm really going to do it." Stabbing the connect button, he barked at whoever was on the other end of the line, "What?"

Angie ducked her head to hide her grin. The original Trident geek loved messing with Ian whenever he was bored or wanting revenge for some reason. Apparently at some point since the phone had last rung, he'd remotely changed the ringtone, and if she knew Brody, he'd made it so Ian couldn't change it back without a new password.

"Shit." A heavy sigh from her husband had her glancing up again to see him stand with a scowl on his face and stalk to the jet's galley. A few of the team members stirred and stretched. When Ian returned moments later with a fresh bottle of water, she wasn't too surprised when he handed it to her. She'd finished the bottle next to her a little while ago, and he was making sure she stayed hydrated.

God, I love this man.

As she mouthed the word "thanks" to him, he checked his military wristwatch and then spoke into the phone. "Fine. We'll be landing in about an hour. Tell Parrish we'll be there at seven." He paused. "Yeah, you and me both. Listen, tell that asshole to change my ringtone back, otherwise I'm finding a reason to send him to the South Pole for a month. Later, bro."

From his last few statements, she'd figured out it was Devon and not his youngest brother, Nick, he'd been talking to. Before she could ask what was wrong, he placed his hands on her chair's arms and leaned down. His lips brushed against hers gently, and she melted as she usually did when he kissed her. His voice dropped, so she was the only one who heard him. "Love you, Angel."

"Love you too, Master Daddy."

One corner of his sexy mouth ticked upward. "Little Bit's got a little brat for a momma, but you're beautiful, so I'll deal with it. That and I love when you're feeling sassy because that means I get to have fun with your punishments. And don't think I forgot about the vibrating anal plug. I decided to wait until your tummy is one hundred percent again."

Angie had been a little nauseous this morning, but thankfully her breakfast and then lunch had stayed down. Of course, she should have known he hadn't forgotten about plugging her ass. She had a love/hate relationship with anal plugs. While wearing one was a literal pain-in-the-ass, they increased the intensity of her orgasms. She let out a tiny snort. "My tummy thanks you, Sir. I just wish my ass could say the same. It would if you gave it a reprieve."

"Not a chance." After another swift kiss, he straightened and pivoted to face the others. "Everyone awake? Good. Just got some bad news—the latest missing submissive was found dead, at an elementary school playground of all fucking places. The FBI is finally . . . *finally* going to use us in a full capacity—they need more undercover people who know the lifestyle. Foster, you'll be joining the Alpha team going into the clubs. McCabe, you too, but you'll be paired with a more experienced agent or cop as your submissive. We'll give you a few one-on-one classes this week so you can pass for a full-fledged Dom. The rest of you will be monitoring the outer perimeters of clubs and getting some training to pass as Doms who aren't in the mood to play, but still look like you know what you're doing inside a club. We've got to nail this fucking bastard.

I'm sick of women being killed, and I'm sick of the submissives in the Tampa area being scared out of their fucking minds."

Putting aside her sketchpad and graphite pencil, Angie stood and wrapped her arms around her husband's waist. As head Dom and co-owner of The Covenant, this was stressing him out more than he was showing to everyone else. The press had recently made the BDSM connection between the murdered women even though the FBI and Tampa PD had done a good job of keeping certain details under wraps. A reporter for the Tampa Bay Times had dubbed the murderer the "Kink Killer," and it had stuck among the media, but most of the local people in the lifestyle refused to use the moniker.

Ian placed his hands over hers on his chest. "On another note, now that we don't have an audience—I have to admit, as much as Shades over there will debate it, I had nothing to do with anything that happened over the past few days. If I was going to screw you over, I would've given you some better competition. But . . ." He chuckled. "All in all, I'm proud of myself."

Her eyes narrowing, Angie peeked around Ian's shoulder. "Of yourself?"

"Damn right. Well, Dev had a little say in it too, but I think I put together a damn good team. I mean, considering what I had to work with . . . seriously, only one frog on the whole fucking team. What the hell was I thinking?"

"You were probably thinking you needed a few Marines to show you how it's done," Abbott quipped. "And a couple of grunts to deal with any big ol' teddy bears we run into."

"Well, at least he added a secret agent man to keep all

you fuckers in line," Foster added, giving them a "Superman" pose with his hands on his hips and his gaze on the cabin's ceiling.

Of course, that kickstarted the banter and jabs among them. Pillows, ice cubes, and anything else they could grab were thrown at each other while ducking what was incoming. They were truly the cohesive team they'd been training to become—they had each other's backs, and most of all, they were now part of the Trident Security family.

Pulling Angie out of the range of flying objects, Ian bent down for another kiss. "Please shoot me if our kids act like this."

"You wouldn't have them any other way."

Continue the adventure with *A Dead Man's Pulse.*
Now available.

I hope you enjoyed *Mountain of Evil* and meeting the new members of the TS Omega Team. For the best reading order of the Trident Security series and its spinoffs, refer to the list on my website.
www.samanthacoleauthor.com

***Denotes titles/series that are available on select digital sites only. Paperbacks and audiobooks are available on most book sites.

THE TRIDENT SECURITY SERIES

Leather & Lace

His Angel

Waiting For Him

Not Negotiable: A Novella

Topping The Alpha

Watching From the Shadows

Whiskey Tribute: A Novella

Tickle His Fancy

No Way in Hell: A Steel Corp/Trident Security Crossover (co-authored with J.B. Havens)

Absolving His Sins

Option Number Three: A Novella

Salvaging His Soul

Trident Security Field Manual

Torn In Half: A Novella

***HEELS, RHYMES, & NURSERY CRIMES SERIES**
(WITH 13 OTHER AUTHORS)
Jack Be Nimble: A Trident Security-Related Short Story

***THE DEIMOS SERIES**
Handling Haven: Special Forces: Operation Alpha
Cheating the Devil: Special Forces: Operation Alpha

THE TRIDENT SECURITY OMEGA TEAM SERIES
Mountain of Evil
A Dead Man's Pulse
Forty Days & One Knight

THE DOMS OF THE COVENANT SERIES
Double Down & Dirty
Entertaining Distraction
Knot a Chance

THE BLACKHAWK SECURITY SERIES
Tuff Enough
Blood Bound

MASTER KEY SERIES
Master Key Resort
Master Cordell

HAZARD FALLS SERIES

Don't Fight It

Don't Shoot the Messenger

THE MALONE BROTHERS SERIES

Take the Money and Run

The Devil's Spare Change

LARGO RIDGE SERIES

Cold Feet

ANTELOPE ROCK SERIES

(CO-AUTHORED WITH J.B. HAVENS)

Wannabe in Wyoming

Wistful in Wyoming

AWARD-WINNING STANDALONE BOOKS

The Road to Solace

Scattered Moments in Time: A Collection of Short Stories & More

*****THE BID ON LOVE SERIES**

(WITH 7 OTHER AUTHORS!)

Going , Going, Gone: Book 2

*****THE COLLECTIVE: SEASON TWO**

(WITH 7 OTHER AUTHORS!)

Angst: Book 7

SPECIAL COLLECTIONS

Trident Security Series: Volume I

USA Today Bestselling Author and Award-Winning Author Samantha Cole is a retired policewoman and former paramedic. Using her life experiences and training, she strives to find the perfect mix of suspense and romance for her readers to enjoy.

Awards:

Wannabe in Wyoming (co-authored by J.B. Havens) won the bronze medal in the 2021 Readers' Favorite Awards in the General Romance category.

Scattered Moments in Time, won the gold medal in the 2020 Readers' Favorite Awards in the Fiction Anthology category.

The Road to Solace (formerly *The Friar*), won the silver medal in the 2017 Readers' Favorite Awards in the Contemporary Romance category.

Samantha has over thirty-five books published throughout several different series as well as a few stand-alone novels. A full list can be found on her website.

Sexy Six-Pack's Sirens Group on Facebook
Website: www.samanthacoleauthor.com
Newsletter: www.geni.us/SCNews

facebook.com/SamanthaColeAuthor
instagram.com/samanthacoleauthor
bookbub.com/profile/samantha-a-cole
goodreads.com/SamanthaCole
tiktok.com/@samanthacoleauthor

www.ingramcontent.com/pod-product-compliance
Lightning Source LLC
Chambersburg PA
CBHW071825190726
48292CB00005B/1606